MR. WHISKERS

and the

Shenanigan Sisters

Also by Wendelin Van Draanen

Flipped

Swear to Howdy

Runaway

The Secret Life of Lincoln Jones

Shredderman

*Shredderman: Secret Identity • Shredderman: Attack of the Tagger
• Shredderman: Meet the Gecko • Shredderman: Enemy Spy*

The Gecko & Sticky

*The Gecko & Sticky: Villain's Lair • The Gecko & Sticky: The Greatest Power •
The Gecko & Sticky: Sinister Substitute • The Gecko & Sticky: The Power Potion*

The Sammy Keyes Mysteries

*Sammy Keyes and the Hotel Thief • Sammy Keyes and the Skeleton
Man • Sammy Keyes and the Sisters of Mercy • Sammy Keyes and the
Runaway Elf • Sammy Keyes and the Curse of Moustache Mary • Sammy
Keyes and the Hollywood Mummy • Sammy Keyes and the Search for
Snake Eyes • Sammy Keyes and the Art of Deception • Sammy Keyes and
the Psycho Kitty Queen • Sammy Keyes and the Dead Giveaway • Sammy Keyes
and the Wild Things • Sammy Keyes and the Cold Hard Cash • Sammy Keyes
and the Wedding Crasher • Sammy Keyes and the Night of Skulls • Sammy
Keyes and the Power of Justice Jack • Sammy Keyes and the Showdown in Sin
City • Sammy Keyes and the Killer Cruise • Sammy Keyes and the Kiss Goodbye*

Van Draanen, Wendelin, author.
Mr. Whiskers and the Shenanigan
sisters
2023
33305255533378
sa   04/12/24

WHISKERS
and the
Shenanigan Sisters

Wendelin Van Draanen
Pictures by Laura Catalán

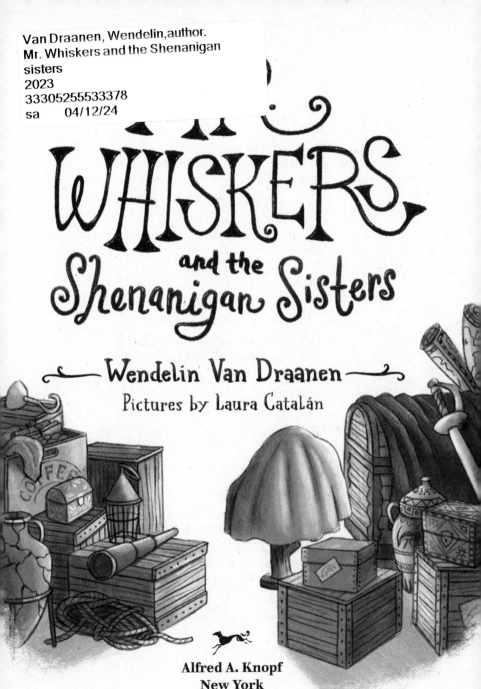

Alfred A. Knopf
New York

THIS IS A BORZOI BOOK PUBLISHED BY ALFRED A. KNOPF

This is a work of fiction. Names, characters, places, and incidents either are the product of the author's imagination or are used fictitiously. Any resemblance to actual persons, living or dead, events, or locales is entirely coincidental.

Text copyright © 2023 by Wendelin Van Draanen
Jacket art and interior illustrations copyright © 2023 by Laura Catalán

All rights reserved. Published in the United States by Alfred A. Knopf, an imprint of Random House Children's Books, a division of Penguin Random House LLC, New York.

Knopf, Borzoi Books, and the colophon are registered trademarks of Penguin Random House LLC.

Visit us on the Web! rhcbooks.com

Educators and librarians, for a variety of teaching tools, visit us at RHTeachersLibrarians.com

Library of Congress Cataloging-in-Publication Data is available upon request.
ISBN 978-0-593-64430-0 (trade) — ISBN 978-0-593-64431-7 (lib. bdg.) — ISBN 978-0-593-64432-4 (ebook)

The text of this book is set in 11.5-point Walbaum Light.
Interior design by Jade Rector

Printed in the United States of America
10 9 8 7 6 5 4 3 2 1
First Edition

Random House Children's Books supports the
First Amendment and celebrates the right to read.

Penguin Random House LLC supports copyright. Copyright fuels creativity, encourages diverse voices, promotes free speech, and creates a vibrant culture. Thank you for buying an authorized edition of this book and for complying with copyright laws by not reproducing, scanning, or distributing any part in any form without permission. You are supporting writers and allowing Penguin Random House to publish books for every reader.

For Barley & Maple,
who know how to make off with the butter!

1
Something Fishy

I smelled trouble. It came driftin' in off a fella on the sidewalk outside and tickled up my schnoz clear down to my paws.

I'd picked up his scent through one of Merryweather Manor's parlor windows. This house is big, old, and drafty, with lots of dark nooks, and furniture for me to hide behind.

And thanks to the ruff way I live?

I've gotten good at hiding.

But I was on the move now, and since the fella was almost out of view, I ditched the parlor, hurried past the library, and slipped into the front room to track him, lettin' out a long, low "Grrrr."

"What's up?" Misty asked from a table near the fireplace, where she and her sister, Zelda, were playing a board game.

Misty's my favorite human. And I knew she was talking to me, but I acted like I didn't so I could keep trackin' the fella from one window to the next.

He was dressed like a cop. Not the uniformed kind. The undercover kind. The kind that would wear dark shades even if the morning fog was still hanging heavy in the air. The kind that's always on high alert.

The trrrouble was, he wasn't *moving* like a cop. He was moving like a sneak thief—something I know more'n a little about, seein' as how I've come foot to fang with quite a few of 'em around town.

Or rather, they've come foot to fang with *me*.

Heh-heh.

Not that anyone's ever put a medal around my neck for helpin' out—actually, quite the opposite. But has that stopped me from takin' a bite out of crime?

Gnaw.

"Grrrr," I said again, 'cause underneath the fella's undercover threads was definitely something fishy. Fishy in a way that's got nothing to do with fins or scales or bulging eyeballs.

Misty was watchin' me, and this time when she spoke, she made sure I knew who she was askin'. "What's wrong, Mr. Whiskers?"

Her callin' me that still makes my chest puff out a little. I like that she bothered to name me, and name me something besides Lousy Mutt or Mangy Mongrel or Scram Ya Scoundrel.

The truth is, Misty Nanigan's the reason I nose my way into the Merryweather so much. This creaky old house has a rep with my street pack for being haunted by ghosts, so I used to steer clear. But since the Nanigans moved in and started slippin' me treats, it's been hard for me to stay away.

Make that impawsible!

I call Misty and Zelda the *She*nanigans, because it fits. That's not *their* fault. What d'ya expect two bored kids stuck in an old house in the middle of a hustle-bustle city to do?

That's rrright—get in trouble.

Their mom's not around, so I don't have a name for her, but I call their dad the *He*nanigan 'cause I'm that kind of funny.

"Mr. Whiskers?" Misty asked again, and this time she stood up.

I gave her a quick pant and a wag of thanks. I like the way she pays attention. I like the way she sticks her nose in, wantin' to know stuff.

"Where are you going?" Zelda asked when Misty started toward me.

The fishy fella was coming up the Merryweather walkway now, so I set my voice lower and louder. *"Grrrr."*

"Someone's here," Misty said, kneeling beside me and stroking my head.

"So what?" Zelda said. "Someone's always coming or going."

"This one's got a funny mustache," Misty said.

See? That girl's sharp as shattered glass. And she was right. Humans do peculiar things with their whiskers, but these were just *wrrrong*—a scraggly patch under his nose. And *crooked* t'boot. Pawthetic.

"What do you think, boy?" Misty asked. "A new boarder?"

The Merryweather is the only house on my rounds where the people living in it are called boarders. It's also the only house where breakfast *and* dinner are served, so I don't care *what* they're called. If there's scraps, I'm all for this bein' a boardinghouse instead of a highfalutin historic hotel. People stay here longer, too, which comes in handy for lyin' low. It's hard work winnin' over new people all the time.

"Aunties!" Zelda called. "Someone's here!" She turned to her sister. "Now will you *please* get back here and finish the game?"

Misty shrugged. "That's okay. I give up."

"What? No!" Zelda cried. Her glasses had slid down her nose, so she pushed them up with a pointer finger and said, "You can't concede!"

Misty kept a sharp eye on the fishy fella as he mounted the steps. "I didn't concede," she muttered. "I just gave up."

"It's the same thing!"

The doorbell chimes went off then, which set *me* off. "Grrr-aarf! Grr-aarf! Grr-aarf-aarf-aarf!"

"Who let that mutt in again?" Auntie Jada asked, tossin' Misty a stern look as she hurried toward the door.

Auntie Jada's the business end of the stick around here, while Auntie Tiana's more the first aid kit. The Aunties aren't related to anyone in the house but each other, but they still want boarders to call them Auntie. "Let's be family," they say anytime someone new moves in. Once, I overheard the Aunties say that making boarders feel like family makes it harder for them to move out. I don't think it's working, though. Movin' out still happens a lot.

Like I said, ghosts.

I wish the Aunties would treat *me* like family, but they don't. I may be "housebroken," but Jada says me bein' inside "breaks house rules."

Crummy rule, if you ask me.

Auntie Jada puts up with me some days because the Nanigans are long-term and she wants them to stay, but most days she gives me the boot. Not mean, like with the highfalutiners—she just uses a broom to scoot me out and tells me to run on home.

I wish.

And c'mon. No collar? No tags? Can't she tell I don't *have* a home?

Auntie Tiana does sometimes sneak me treats out the back door. "He'll never leave if you do that," Jada scolds her, but Tiana just gives me a wink, which she never notices I give back.

Tiana was nowhere to be seen right now, though, which was actually fine by me. This fishy fella needed to be handled by someone rrrough and tough, and if they weren't gonna let me at him, Jada was the Auntie for the job.

Except that right now Jada wasn't worried about the fishy fella at her front door.

She was worried about me.

"Girls," Jada snapped. "Ms. LeTrist is in the library trying to work. I can't have all this noise! Put Whiskey outside, and then either play down here *quietly* or go to your quarters!"

I don't mind that Jada calls me Whiskey. I like Mr. Whiskers best, but Whiskey's still a whole lot better'n Lousy Mutt or Mangy Mongrel or Scram Ya Scoundrel.

So Misty scooped me up like she was followin' Jada's orders. And since she was actin' like she really *was* gonna toss me out back, I gave her my best puppy look.

"Don't worry," she whispered. "Just hush, okay?" Then she ducked into an alcove and crouched in the space between the wall and a big display case—a place my nose said had a history of upchuck and cat.

Zelda crammed in next to us but wasn't happy about it. "Why do you always want to spy on people?" she grumbled.

"Why *don't* you want to?" Misty asked back.

"Because it gets us in trouble! I'm eleven years old now. I can't be *spying* on people."

"Well, I'm ten," Misty said, "and I can."

Right then the front door opened and a strong whiff of fishy whooshed in.

"Grrr," I said. I swear it was under my breath, but Misty gave me a little shake to remind me to be quiet.

I licked her face, tellin' her I was sorry. The truth is, I'm still gettin' the hang of spying. Of lyin' low instead of charging. Of perkin' an ear without making a peep.

Spying's *ruff*.

Fishy's voice drifted into the alcove. "Morning, ma'am. I'm looking for Professor Felix Nanigan."

Misty scooted toward the edge of the wall, and we both peeked around at Fishy, who had worked his way inside. He was taller'n Jada by a head, but not nearly as wide. And it didn't take a watchdog to notice he was sniffin' the joint.

"And you are?" Jada asked, her eyes narrowing like she was smellin' something fishy, too.

The man flashed a badge. "FBI."

Misty and Zelda looked at each other. "The FBI?" Zelda mouthed. *"Why?"*

Misty's eyes slowly rose into full moons. And I must have some husky in me, 'cause I had a furocious urge to howl! "Uh-oh," she said.

"What?" Zelda whispered.

Misty shook her head. "Nothing."

But I could see that she *did* know something.

And that whatever it was, wasn't good.

2
Dadnapped

"What do you know that I don't?" Zelda asked.

"Shh!" Misty whispered, her eyes on Auntie Jada, who was pulling a phone from her pocket.

"I'll text the professor," Jada told Fishy, then jabbed around the phone with her thumbs.

The phone zwooped.

She waited.

It pinged.

She stared at it.

I hate phones. I can never tell what's goin' on.

"He says he'll be right down," Jada told Fishy.

I like the Henanigan. He smells like tall grass mixed with elm bark, and he knows how to grow whiskers. His head and his whole *face* know how. The dog's honest truth is, I'm a little jealous.

The Henanigan also slips me treats at dinner when I manage to sneak under the table without the Aunties noticing. Belle LeTrist isn't nice like that. She only ever serves me a swipe of shoe. And the new fella, Brian Bunker, he's a croaky old toad who doesn't understand a friendly nudge or ever say much more'n "Pass the rolls."

In any case, while we were waitin' on the Henanigan to come downstairs, Zelda tried again. "Misty, why won't you tell me?"

"Because you'll make fun of me."

"I will not!" Zelda said, sounding like *she'd* been swiped with a shoe.

Misty sighed. "It's probably nothing."

Two floors up I heard boards creak along the hallway.

"*What's* probably nothing?" Zelda whispered.

"Shh!" Misty hissed. "You'll get us caught."

The stairs groaned and squeaked until the footsteps were only one floor up.

"Where *is* he?" Fishy demanded.

How could he not know?

Humans and their little ears.

Pitiful.

Jada peered up the stairwell. "He's coming," she assured him.

And then there he was, with his hair stickin' out every which way, lookin' like a sheep that had lost his flock.

I must have some border collie in me, 'cause I had the sudden urge to run out and nip his heels.

"Hello, I'm Felix Nanigan," the professor said. "Jada says you're with the FBI? What's this about?"

"You know what it's about, Professor," Fishy said. "I'm afraid I'm going to have to take you in."

"Take me in? Why?"

"Do you really want me to say?" Fishy asked.

"Yes!"

"Are you *sure*?" Fishy leaned back and smirked at us peeking around the wall. "In front of your *kids*?"

The Henanigan spotted us and froze. He looked like one of those statues in the park that pigeons perch on to poop.

"Don't worry, girls," he finally said. "I'm sure it's a simple misunderstanding. Stay here with Auntie Jada, and I'll be back in a jiff." He turned to Fishy and said, "I'll just grab a few things and—"

Fishy latched on to his arm. "Do you have your keys?"

"Yes, but—"

Fishy pushed him along by the shoulder. "Then you're coming, and you're coming now."

"What?" the professor said, struggling a little. "*Why?*"

Fishy was pawin' through a pocket with his free hand. "Because you're classified as a flight risk."

"A *flight* risk?" the professor asked.

Quicker'n a snakebite, Fishy had the professor's wrists clamped together with a plastic zip tie.

"What are you doing?" the professor barked. "I'm an archeology professor at the college! I'm a single dad! My girls are here! I'm not a flight risk!"

"I can vouch for all of that," Jada said, movin' quick to block the front door.

"What you can do, ma'am," Fishy said, "is get out

of my way." Then he bumped her aside and muscled the Henanigan outside.

Misty scooped me up and ran for the door. "Daddy!" she yelped. "What's going on?"

"I'll call as soon as I can," the professor shouted over his shoulder. "The Aunties are in charge. Mind them!"

I was a pretty big load for Misty, but she held on tight as we watched Fishy hustle the Henanigan out to a car that was double-parked on the street. There was a driver waiting behind the wheel.

"I thought the FBI used black SUVs," Zelda said,

her eyes pinching down. "So why's he taking Dad over to a Prius?"

"And look!" Misty cried as she and Zelda moved toward the street. "It has Uber and Lyft stickers!"

"Girls! Go upstairs!" the Henanigan shouted from the curb. "Do things *by the book*, and remember to *earn* your way!" His voice sounded different now. Urgent. "It's how doors will open for you!"

"What?" Zelda asked.

"Misty! Zelda!" Jada called from the porch. "You heard your daddy—come inside!"

"But that guy's pushing Daddy into a *Prius*!"

"Girls!" Jada called.

"Help!" Misty screamed as the car rolled forward, and I answered the call. I squirmed out of her arms and tore down the sidewalk, chasin' after the Henanigan. I ran for block after block, as fast as I could, jumpin' and weavin' and divin' between legs like I was winning Westminster. I got honked at and yelled at and called some hair-raisin' names, but I didn't let it slow me down. I charged ahead so fast that even my tongue couldn't keep up!

And I *was* gaining on the car, too, but after it turned into Golden Gate Park, something happened that tripped up my concentration.

A phone flew out the window.

It sailed through the air in front of me and landed with a swoosh in a bush.

My head went back and forth between the bush and the car.

Was it the Henanigan's phone?

I must have some golden in me, 'cause I really, really, *really* wanted to retrieve that phone! But . . . hauling it along while I chased the car?

It would be too hard to breathe.

So instead of fetchin' the phone, I marked the bush with a quick squirt and kept running.

The fly in the kibble was, that little stop 'n' spray cost me. The car had pulled way ahead, and once it was out of the park, it zigged and zagged through streets faster'n a whippet, and I lost it.

I had no idea where the car was going, but there *was* one thing I knew fur-sure:

The Henanigan had been dadnapped!

3
Let Me In!

I marked my turnaround spot and lots of other poles as I traced my steps back to the Merryweather. Not a lot, okay? Just enough so it'd be easy to find my way again. Like I did with the phone. Do you know how many plants there are in Golden Gate Park? Do you know how many dogs trot through there, markin' their path? Do you know how ruff it would have been to find the phone bush without leavin' my own scent?

Well, be a dog for a day and you'll get the whole squirting thing. We may not have eyes as sharp as yours, or see colors the way you do, but our nose tells us a million things in the time it takes you to blink. We've got whole maps laid out in our brains.

Maps drawn by what we smell, and every time we sniff, it's to update the map. Who's been here? How long ago? Friend or foe?

The nose knows.

So, I may have lost the car, but I found the phone, and by the time I'd nudged my way through the Merryweather's back door, my paws were sore and I was thirsty.

Inside the back hallway I put down the phone and called, "Aarf! Aarf!" which is code for *Emergency! Come quick!* in case you didn't know.

Which, apparently, Auntie Jada didn't. She acted like it meant *Come at me with a broom,* 'cause that's what she did, saying, "Shoo! Git!"

Auntie Tiana put herself in between us. "I'll deal with him," she said. Tiana was smaller than her sister but had a calming power over her—and everyone else, too. I couldn't really put a paw on why, but she could be like a warm blanket when you hadn't figured out yet that you were cold.

In any case, Tiana gave Jada a rub on the arms and said, "You get back to paying the bills."

"I'd rather deal with *him*," Jada said with a sigh. "We have *got* to find a way out of this mess."

"We will," Tiana said, tossin' on the invisible blanket.

"We can't afford to lose the Nanigans!" Jada whispered.

"We won't. You'll see. Everything'll be fine."

The instant Jada was gone, I nudged the phone toward Tiana. "Aarf! Aarf!"

"What's this?" she said, bendin' over to pick it up. But then she pulled a face and said, "Ew!"

Okay, yeah, it was drippin' with slobber, but what do you expect? It's how I sweat, and there's lots of hills in San Francisco! Which I'd just run at full speed! Because, like I said, emergency!

"Aarf! Aarf!"

"Whose is this, boy?" Tiana said, headin' into the kitchen with the phone.

You're kidding, right? I answered. *Can't you smell him?*

It came out: "Aarf! Aarf! . . . Aarf! Aarf! Aarf!"

She looked at me suspiciously. "You're not a pick-pocket, are you?"

A pickpocket? No! Well . . . yes, but not this time! It's the Henanigan's! You know . . . the professor's?

That also came out as "Aarf! Aarf! . . . Aarf! Aarf! Aarf!" with an extra "Aarf-aarf-aarf-aarf-aarf-aarf-aarf!"

"Hmm." She tapped and prodded the thing while she muttered about passwords and police and what to do. Finally she slipped it inside a plastic bag and put it in a drawer. "Well, for now we'll just hope someone comes to claim it."

"Aarf! Aarf! Aarf!" I cried, shakin' my head and wigglin' my whole body.

It obviously meant *No! That's NOT what we should do!* but Jada was back, and she was done with me and my noise. "Go home, Whiskey!" she said, grabbin' the broom. "We can't afford to have you making such a racket!"

This time Tiana didn't stand in the way. "I've really got to get to the market," she said, washing her hands at the sink.

I dodged Jada. I couldn't leave now! I had to find the Shenanigans and let them know about the phone! I tore through the house, back and forth, all around, lookin' for Misty and Zelda, while Jada chased me with the broom. "Get out of my parlor!" Jada hissed, tryin' not to disturb Belle LeTrist.

So I got out of the parlor . . . and charged up the stairs!

"Whiskey!" she called after me. "Whiskey, you get back here this instant!"

I'd never been to the Nanigans' apartment or even up the Merryweather's stairs, but the old carpet runner gave me great traction, and since the Aunties aren't exactly quick on the risers, I was hopin' I could find Misty and Zelda before Jada caught me.

And I was just about at the second-floor landing when, in a rare stroke of good luck, the front door chimes went off.

"Oh, you little rascal," I heard Jada mutter as she gave up the chase to answer the door.

When I got to the third floor, my nose went on the hunt. It led me down the hallway to the last door, where I whimpered and whined, hopin' the Shenanigans would hear me.

Nobody opened the door.

So I pawed at the door while I whimpered and whined a little louder.

Still no answer.

So I barked. "Aarf! Aarf! . . . Aarf! Aarf!" Then I pawed at the door and whimpered and whined even *louder*.

And finally!

"Mr. Whiskers!" Misty said. "What are you doing up here?" She leaned out and checked the hallway. "You can come in, but you need to be quiet. *Really* quiet, okay?"

I panted and nodded, showin' her I understood.

"Good boy. Come in."

As I followed her, I noticed she smelled different. Nervous. With a dash of fear. She'd never smelled this way before, and it worried me a little.

But then I turned into the living room and got distracted by everything around me.

You know how I said the Merryweather is old? Well, it's not just the house and the furniture. It's *everything* inside it. The drapes, the wallpaper, the carpets, the clocks that gong and ping and chime, the paintings of big ships with sails, men with swords, and women wearin' frills and *foxes*. Even the dishes the Aunties use at dinner look like they're a hundred years old.

Make that *seven* hundred if you're countin' in canine.

But the Aunties sure seem to like their house and everything in it. They tell stories at dinner sometimes, especially the first night someone new moves in. One of the Aunties will point to a portrait of a pirate who's holdin' a sword in the air and has one boot planted on top of a treasure chest and say, "Our great-great-great-great-granddaddy was Mad-Eye Mick—a fearsome pirate who sailed the seven seas in search of treasure. Folks say he was the deadliest man on water, but fate shipwrecked him right off the coast here. And when our great-great-great-great-grandmamma Rose caught his eye, why, he gave up his swashbucklin' and built her this very house, which included a saloon for him and his salty mates to enjoy. You're sitting in what used to be the saloon!" And no matter where the story went from there, they always wound things down with "Oh, the tales these walls could tell."

I'm all for hearin' the Aunties' stories again and again, 'cause when they're yappin' about pirates and old saloons, it's easy to nudge tasty scraps out of people around the table.

In any case, as old as everything in the house is and smells, it was brand-new, uptown shiny compared with what I was seein' and smellin' in the Nanigans' quarters. There were old maps on the walls, a tall piano, stacks and stacks of books, and scrolls of briny-smellin' paper. Off to one side was a big, messy desk planted like a seawall in front of a bookcase. The bottom half of each wall was covered in wood paneling, and the top half had faded wallpaper that was peelin' in places. And the rugs! They had the most complicated smell I'd ever come across and were older'n the dirt ground into them.

I gave everything a good sniff 'n' snuff, making a mental map out of the main room. Everything might have been old, but at least some of the furniture looked comfortable. Downstairs it was all small and hard. Up here there was an overstuffed chair and a long couch that would be great for snoozin'. If I ever got a chance to stay that long.

I took a detour into the bathroom, and while I was there, I lapped up half the toilet bowl. I was *that* thirsty. It went down easy, too. Don't judge.

I also checked out the two bedrooms. The Shenanigans' was small and tidy, and it smelled so good—just like Misty and Zelda—and their beds were covered in fluffy pillows and fuzzy blankets and way too many teddy bears.

Boneheaded to be jealous of stuffed toys, I know, but I was.

In any case, the other bedroom was a mess and smelled like sheep.

I knew whose that was!

My nose was about done mapping things when my ears perked at the sound of the Shenanigans whisperin' in the main room.

I trotted back and found Zelda standing in front of a bricked-over fireplace. "Look," she was sayin', "maybe the Aunties couldn't reach him by phone or get through to the FBI, but why won't they call the police?"

"Isn't the FBI the police, only . . . stronger?" Misty asked. "So wouldn't that be like calling the police on the police?"

Zelda heaved a sigh. "I guess. But . . . isn't there *anything* we can do?"

"Maybe we should figure out what Daddy was trying to tell us," Misty said. "It was like the riddles he does with us sometimes, don't you think?"

Zelda nodded, then said, "'Do things *by the book* . . . remember to *earn* your way. . . .'" She nudged her glasses up. "What was the third part?"

"'It's how doors will open for you,'" Misty said. Then she added, "He also said, 'Go upstairs,' so it has to be in here, right?"

Zelda nodded and muttered, "Whatever *it* is."

They both started scanning the room, mutterin', "'Do things by the book . . . remember to *earn* your way. . . . It's how doors will open for you. . . . Do things by the book . . . remember to *earn* your way. . . . It's how doors will open for you. . . .'"

It sounded like a swarm of bees, and since bees can be, well, *beestly*, I was about to lie down and cover my ears when Misty gasped.

"What?" Zelda asked.

Misty's eyes were fixed on the fireplace mantel behind Zelda, and they were going full moon. "'*Earn* your way,'" she said, pointing at an old lidded vase that had four funny feet. She began to pant a little. Like she was having trouble breathing. "That's an *urn*," she whispered, and I caught a whiff of about-to-faint.

I leapt over to Misty to break her fall or lick her face or help *somehow* if she went down, but she snapped to and went to grab the funny-footed urn.

Zelda beat her to it. "An *urn*," she whispered, holding it.

I nuzzled in and tried to give the urn a sniff. Metals are harder to read than most things, and this fancy chunk of it was no exception.

Zelda pulled off the lid and looked inside.

"What's in it?" Misty asked.

Zelda frowned and shook the urn upside down. "Nothing."

"Nothing?" Misty grabbed it, but Zelda didn't let go. "Hey," Misty said, holding the funny-footed bottom end. "It was my idea!"

"But there's nothing in it," Zelda said, and since she wasn't letting go, Misty tried to twist it free.

Instead the funny-footed bottom twisted right off.

"Oh no!" Misty cried. But then she saw something inside the funny-footed bottom, and her eyes went full howlin' moon.

"Oh!" she whispered, reaching inside. "Oh my golly gosh!"

4
Quick, Hide!

I stretched up onto my hind legs to see what Misty was oh-my-golly-goshing about and watched her unclamp something from inside the urn's funny-footed bottom. "Wow . . . ," she said, holding it up. "A skeleton key!"

A *skeleton* key? My schnoz went to work, but . . . it sure didn't *smell* like bone. It smelled like . . . rust and . . . the Henanigan?

Zelda blinked at the key. "But . . . what in the world does it go to?"

"Must go to some kind of a door, right?" Misty answered, but her eyes had gone shifty.

Which made Zelda's eyes pinch down to slits behind her glasses.

It's a hair-raisin' look on her.

Very catlike.

"What are you not telling me?" Zelda asked. "I *promise* I won't make fun of you."

Misty sank into the overstuffed chair with a big sigh. "Three nights ago a noise woke me up, so I came out here, and I *swear* I saw the bookcase move. Dad was standing right by it and told me to go back to bed. He laughed when I asked why the bookcase had moved, and said I must have been dreaming. But I . . . I swear I saw it move!"

"Move how?"

"It just *moved.* But only a little."

Zelda took a deep breath. "Okaaay . . . and what happened after that?"

"I couldn't get back to sleep, so after Daddy went to bed, I got up and tried to move the bookcase. I tried everything but couldn't get it to budge."

"So . . . maybe you *were* dreaming?" Zelda said.

Misty shrugged. "Or maybe that key has something to do with opening it. Daddy *knows* I saw it move. And he was trying to tell us *something.*"

Zelda nodded. "And he did say, 'Do things by the

book,' so maybe the door that will open for us is *by* the *book*case."

Misty shivered. "I feel like I'm in a spooky old movie."

Zelda frowned. "Well, this *is* a spooky old house."

They went over to the bookcase, and you bet yer bacon I followed. And while they shoved it and pulled it and dug around in the shelves, I patrolled it with my nose.

It didn't take long for me to figure out that the professor had spent a lot of time touchin' one side of the bookcase and that there was a draft comin' from behind it. A cool, musty breeze with traces of mold, wood rot, and mice. So I began pawin' and snortin' at the narrow space between the wall and the bookcase.

"What is it, boy?" Misty asked, and inspected where I was pawing. "Zelda!" she whispered. "There's a draft!"

I got so excited she understood me that my tail went wild. I tried to stop it because—as the Aunties can tell you—it causes trouble. Unfortunately, the thing's got a mind of its own, and now, as usual when everything was going great, it turned into a hairy propeller, and this time it knocked over an umbrella stand.

It scared me as much as it did Misty and Zelda. We all jumped and spun around, and I wanted to say I was sorry, but I stopped myself in the nick of time. Usually, apologizin' gets me booted, because for some reason people don't like bein' licked when you've just broken something, even though I'm just sayin', *Sorry-sorry-sorry!*

So instead I made myself sit real still while I gave Misty a hangdog look through my lashes. Only she wasn't payin' any attention to me. She was pointing at the floor where the umbrella stand had been. "Zelda!" she gasped. "Look!"

I looked, too. And right there, gapin' up at us from the wooden floor, was a small slot that was rounded on one end.

"A keyhole?" Zelda whispered. "In the *floor*?" And then, because we were all just staring at it, she said, "Well? What are we waiting for?"

So Misty put the key into the slot.

My ears perked at the sound of metal on metal.

Then Misty turned the key and . . . *ka-thunk* . . . the bookcase seemed to give a sigh of relief.

We looked at each other with wide eyes.

"Shut *up*," Zelda said.

Misty slipped the key into her pocket. "What in the world was Daddy up to?"

My ears perked again, but at a different sound.

A watch-out sound.

Footsteps.

I nosed Misty, but she ignored me. So I nudged her again, this time harder.

"What is it, boy?"

A knock at the door answered for me.

The Shenanigans gasped and looked at each other. And then we heard a man's voice say, "Lady, move aside. I have a search warrant."

It wasn't Fishy's voice, but something told me this fella and Fishy swam in the same shady sea.

"Oh my golly gosh," Misty whispered.

"Is this even his room?" a different voice asked. It was a lady. Not one of the Aunties. And even from those few words I could tell—she wasn't the sharpest claw on the paw.

"Of course it is!" Jada snarled.

"Then why's that plaque say 'Captain's Quarters'?" the lady said like she was pouncin' on a lie. "Shouldn't it be 'Professor's Quarters'?"

"Oh, for Mick's sake," Jada moaned. "Are you really asking that?" Then, without waiting for an answer, she snapped, "Let me see that warrant again. And your badge!"

There was a real growl to Jada's voice, which gave me courage. I spun around and nosed the corner of the bookcase where the Henanigan's scent was. The draft comin' from behind the bookcase was stronger now. We had to figure out how to open it, or lock it again before the apartment door opened.

Zelda seemed to be thinkin' the same thing. She turned around and pushed sideways on the bookcase.

It didn't budge.

I pawed and nosed at the slit between the wall and the bookcase where the draft was strongest.

And when Zelda caught on, she pried her fingers in the slit and pulled.

The bookcase groaned.

And creaked.

And then . . . it swung toward us like a door.

5
The Secret Room

The Shenanigans and I stared at a dark, gaping hole in the wall. Cool air swept out of it.

Zelda opened the bookcase door a little wider. Behind it was some sort of room, crowded with musty-smellin' stuff. I could see wooden crates, a camera clamped to a stand above a small table, and something the shape of a toy chest covered by an old blanket.

"What *is* this place?" Zelda asked. There was a heavy black cloth hangin' by two grommets over the back wall. It looked like a flag but with no design. Just black, with edges shredded like a cat had clawed it.

A loud knock at the front door goosed all of us. "Girls?" Auntie Jada called through the wood. "Open up."

"What do we do?" Misty asked, and now the whiff off her was *fear.*

"Girls!" Jada's voice called again. "I'm sorry, but I'm going to have to open the door myself if you don't answer!"

Quicker than a snapped towel, Zelda grabbed Misty by the wrist and dragged her into the secret room. I leapt in behind them, and Zelda pulled a handle on the back of the bookcase, shutting us inside.

It was just in the nick of time, too. "Misty? Zelda?" Jada's voice called, this time from inside the apartment.

We held real still. Light seeped in through cracks in the back of the bookcase, and there was more comin' in through some sort of hole in the wall near the ceiling.

After a little while Zelda whispered, "Wow. A secret room!"

"But whose stuff is this?" Misty whispered. "Is it Daddy's? And what's this camera doing here like this?"

The camera was pointin' straight down at the little table, which *was* a head-scratcher.

"I have no idea," Zelda said. She reached for a long metal tube that went up to the hole in the wall. "Is this a . . . ?" She put her eye up to the curved end and gasped. "It is! It's a periscope!"

"Shh!" Misty hissed, and Zelda hissed back, "Sorry!"

A couple of wags later, Zelda whispered, "Oh, wow. I can see everything through this! Jada's in there with a man and a lady cop."

Misty put her eye up to one of the cracks in the wall, and I found a crack of my own to look through. The lady's hair was pulled back in a poodle puff, and her uniform was hangin' loose as a shar-pei's coat.

"I don't think those are real cops," Misty whispered. "See their shoes?"

She was right—there was nothin' coplike about 'em. They were runners. Runners that had seen a lot of miles.

The man had a long, pointy nose and was lookin' around like a twitchy rat. "This is going to take a while," he was sayin' to Jada. "You can stay, but you probably have better things to do. We'll check in with you before we leave."

"But . . . what exactly are you looking for?" Jada asked.

"I'm afraid the professor was trading in stolen artifacts," the woman said. "Things he was trying to sell on the black market." She gave Jada a keen look. "Know anything about some old gold coins?"

"Gold coins?" Jada asked.

"That's right," Rat Man said. "If you do, you should say. You don't want to be an accomplice in this."

"I don't know anything about gold coins," Jada said. "And I don't believe that he does, either. The man studies old bones and broken pottery, for Mick's sake."

"What about his daughters?" Rat Man said.

Jada called out, "Girls! If you're in here, show yourselves! I don't care that you've got Whiskey, just come out!"

Poodle Puff and Rat Man exchanged looks. Then Poodle Puff raised an eyebrow at Jada. "You don't care that they've got *whiskey*?"

Jada snorted, pulled out her phone, and sat down in the overstuffed chair. "Not what it sounds like."

Somewhere in the distance a phone rang.

I recognized the Henanigan's ring-a-ling-a-ling.

Jada was trying to call him.

I looked from Misty to Zelda, but neither of them seemed to hear it, which made me so furrustrated that I almost yipped.

"Look!" Misty whispered. She was pointin' at a keyhole in the floor, just like the one outside.

"It locks from the inside, too?" Zelda breathed.

Misty nodded. "Looks like. Should I try?"

"Yes!"

"What if it goes *thunk*?"

"I'll watch and see if anyone notices," Zelda whispered. "But I sure don't want them finding this hiding place. Or us!"

So Misty put the skeleton key in the hole, twisted it, and *thunk,* the lock turned and the bookcase shuddered.

"That was so loud!" Misty whispered.

"They didn't notice," Zelda said. "They're too busy digging through Dad's stuff." She turned away from the periscope and pointed to the thing that was shaped like a toy chest. "What do you think's under that blanket?"

So Misty pulled the blanket off.

Only it wasn't a toy chest.

"Oh, wow!" Zelda cried, then slapped a hand over her mouth 'cause she hadn't exactly whispered.

Misty gasped. "Is that a . . . *treasure* chest?"

I nosed in. The lid was rounded and held closed with long, buckled leather straps. It smelled like sea and sea*weed* and sea*gulls* and—

"Hey," Misty said, "is this the same treasure chest that's in the Mad-Eye Mick portrait in the dining room?"

The girls moon-eyed each other.

They moon-eyed the chest.

"Should we open it?" Zelda whispered. "Do you think there's . . . *gold coins* inside it?"

"Maybe . . . ?" Misty said, but neither of them budged.

So I nudged a leather strap and tossed them a look that said, *Snap to it, Shenanigans!*

"I swear that dog understands us," Zelda muttered. She pushed up her glasses, knelt in front of the chest, unbuckled the straps, and pulled up the lid.

The hinges went *creeeeak.*

Zelda froze.

Waited.

Then . . . *creeeak.*

"Let's wait until they're gone!" Misty whispered.

But the lid was up high enough to look inside now, so I nosed right up to it and . . . *woofer,* what a complicated smell! Wood, sure. Sea salt, definitely. Paper and mold and mice, yip. But there was also blood. And hangin' like a nasty bottom burp over all of it was the lip-curlin' odor of death.

I took a step back. If this chest could talk, I'm not sure I'd want to hear the tales it had to tell.

Zelda didn't seem to notice the smell. She held the lid up with one hand and stuck her head right under it. "There's old maps . . . ," she muttered. "A telescope . . ." She pulled out a sword. "And this!"

Misty took the sword and turned it back and forth. "It looks like the sword in that dining room painting!" she whispered. "So . . . do you think there really was a Mad-Eye Mick? Do you think this is . . . *his* stuff?"

"If it is, it's a big letdown," Zelda said, her head buried inside the chest. "I'm not seeing gold, or jewels, or *anything* valuable in it."

Misty put down the sword. "Well, forget about it, then. We're trying to help Daddy, remember? Maybe there's some clues in these crates."

So Misty went over to inspect them, and a few wags later she whispered, "Hey! I found a head lamp! And look—Daddy's Goldie Bear beanie!"

"We're looking for gold, not Goldie," Zelda said, still diggin' through the chest.

Misty frowned and got back to work.

Next she found gloves.

Then a dark, thick sweatshirt.

I gave them all a quick sniff.

Yip. Henanigan.

"Why are these back here?" Misty whispered. "What has Daddy been *doing*?"

It was a good question. I'd pegged the Henanigan as a tired sheep, but all of this was proving me wrong. Maybe he just wore a sheepy disguise. Maybe he was really a *wolf.*

"There's something . . . ," Misty said, gropin' around the sweatshirt. Then she unzipped one of the pockets and pulled out a little drawstring pouch.

My nose told me the pouch was leather. Sea-salty. Old.

My *ears* told me there was something metal inside.

Zelda must've heard it, too, because now she *was* looking. "Is it . . . ?"

So Misty opened the drawstring and . . .

Turned the pouch out into her hand and . . .

Good grrravy.

It *was* gold!

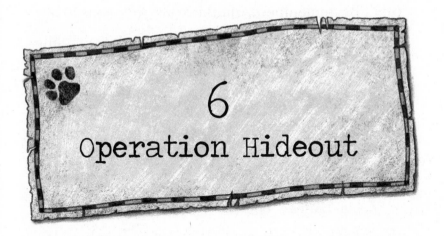

6
Operation Hideout

"Oh my golly gosh!" Misty whispered. "It's old coins!"

"And they're *gold*," Zelda gasped, her eyes shiny with excitement.

Misty's eyes went watery. "Why were these in Daddy's sweatshirt? Was he *taking* them? What kind of trouble is he *in*?"

I hurried over and licked her hand, and Zelda sat next to her and whispered, "Dad's not a thief, he's an archeology professor. He's a nerd who likes old stuff."

"But what if he likes something enough to steal it? What if that's why the FBI came?"

Zelda put an arm around Misty. "It wasn't the

real FBI, remember? And those are *fake* cops in our apartment. *They're* the criminals, not Dad!" She took the coins from Misty and inspected them. "But wow. These *are* really old. And probably worth a lot. This one says 1778!"

"So these *must* be what they're after, right?" Misty whispered.

Zelda handed her the coins and nodded. "Put them back in the sweatshirt and hide it behind the crates. We don't want to be caught with them, and we don't want anyone else to find them!"

Zelda hurried over to the periscope, but Misty just sat staring at the Henanigan's stuff. Finally she took in a deep breath, pulled the Goldie Bear beanie onto her head, and put the pouch back inside the sweatshirt pocket. But once the pouch was in the pocket, she pulled something else out of it.

I moved in for a sniff. It was a small card, but I couldn't map much from it before Misty slipped it into her own pocket and told me, "Shh," like her havin' the card was our little secret. Then she hid the sweatshirt behind the crates and went over to

Zelda, who had one eye up to the periscope. "What do you see?"

"They're tearing the place apart!" Zelda whispered. "But Jada's keeping an eye on them."

"Well, if they're *criminals*," Misty said, "we need to get out of here and call the police!"

Suddenly Zelda said, "Shh!" and her hand flapped like the wing of an angry seagull.

A half flap later Rat Man's voice came through the wall. "Did you hear that?" he said.

"Hear what?" Poodle Puff asked.

"Voices!"

I spied through a crack. Rat Man was creepin' around the desk like he was ready to pounce.

Jada was still in the chair. "Oh, we've got ghosts," she said. "You feel that cool draft?"

Rat Man looked around nervously.

"That's them," Jada said. "You hear them and feel them all hours of the day and night." She glanced at him. "You get used to it." Then she stood and said, "So can we wrap this up? Looks like you're finding a whole lot of nothing. And really, the professor's not the kind of guy who'd be dealing black market. He's very quiet. Follows the rules. Reads *books*."

"We're just getting started," Poodle Puff said. She looked up from a framed picture she'd been studying on the Henanigan's desk. "And you're not going to scare us off by talking about *ghosts*."

Jada shrugged and sat back down. "Well, I'm staying for the duration. I'm not letting you toss the place."

"It might be hours," Poodle Puff warned.

"Hours?" Zelda mouthed. "We might be stuck in here for *hours*?"

I *was* feeling pretty caged. Trapped, even. Also, I more'n kinda had to lift a leg.

I probably shouldn't have half emptied the bowl.

To get my mind off that business, I turned it back to other business. With the tizzy over treasure, I'd kinda forgotten about the *draft*. But Jada mentionin' ghosts had reminded me, and now I couldn't help wonderin' why there was a draft at all. We were in a closed, dark box, so . . . where was it coming from?

My nose tracked the stream of air to the back wall—to the big tattered flag that hung over most of it. I nose-nudged the flag. It was heavier than it looked, and smelled like . . . fog. But I was sure the draft was driftin' from behind it, so I worked my head between the flag and the wall, and . . .

I jumped back quick!

I almost barked, too, but muzzled myself in the nick of time.

Was that a . . . ?

Noooo.

Couldn't be!

I nosed back the foggy flag again and . . .

Jumped back again!

I was dyin' to bark, or just *attack*, but I didn't want to compromise Operation Hideout, so I leapt back to Misty, gripped her pant leg in my teeth, and pulled.

"Stop!" she hissed. "What are you doing?"

I backpawed, not letting go.

Finally she gave in and let me pull her along to the back wall, where I let go of her pants and nosed behind the foggy flag.

She took a peek behind it and . . .

Jumped back!

"Oh my golly gosh!" she gasped.

Zelda was with us now. "What's going on?"

Misty slowly pulled the cloth aside. Zelda looked behind it and . . .

Jumped back!

"Is it . . . alive?" she asked, barely breathing.

"It hasn't moved yet," Misty whispered, "so . . . no?"

Well, I know a big-beaked crow when I see one, and with its head cocked a little to one side, and the way it was perched on a long peg stickin' out from one of the wooden beams that framed the house, it sure *looked* real.

But it didn't move. Didn't twitch a feather.

Finally Zelda said, "It's stuffed."

"But . . . why's it here?" Misty asked.

We all nosed in closer, and that's when we saw that the crow was guardin' steps that curved down and around, disappearin' into darkness.

"A spiral staircase?" Zelda whispered. "What in the world . . . ?"

The staircase steps were small, narrow, and *really* steep. Just looking down them was makin' me pant, and not in a good way. If ya gotta know the dog's honest truth, I'm a cowardly canine when it comes to steep stairs. Going up's okay, but down? With my tail shootin' up and the rest of me nose-divin'? The Chihuahua in me freaks out and I feel like I'm gonna die.

Misty's eyes had gone full moons again. "So you think those stories the Aunties tell at dinner are actually *true*?" she whispered. "I thought they were all made up! I thought *everything* was made up!"

"I thought so, too!" Zelda said. "Dad said they tell those stories to make the house seem cool, so people won't complain about the drafts and creaky floors and scary sounds."

"But this secret room . . . that treasure chest . . . so there really *was* a Mad-Eye Mick?" Misty whispered.

Zelda let out a little gust of air. "It's sure looking like it."

"Do you think he used to hide out back here?" Misty asked.

Zelda scratched her head. "Maybe he missed being a pirate? Maybe this is his . . . his crow's nest or something?"

We were all quiet for a few wags, then Misty whispered, "The whole thing's creepy. And where do those steps *go*? Do you think Daddy . . . ?"

"Went down them?" Zelda asked. "Like, to sneak around at night?"

"I hate this! I hate all of this!" Misty whimpered.

"Gold coins? A secret room? A treasure chest?" Zelda shrugged. "I wouldn't say I hate any of this!"

"But Daddy's in trouble!" Misty said. "We need to find him! And if he went down those steps . . . maybe *we* should, too. Maybe it'll tell us something."

"But . . . it's really dark! And we have no idea where they go."

I was definitely on Zelda's side.

Going down those stairs?

It might snuff me out for good.

"Well, we can't wait in here for hours," Misty whispered, grabbing the head lamp and strapping it on over the Goldie Bear beanie. "Daddy's in trouble *now*."

Zelda frowned.

She crossed her arms.

She frowned harder.

And just when I thought she was gonna save me from those Doomsday Stairs, she said, "Okay. Let's do this."

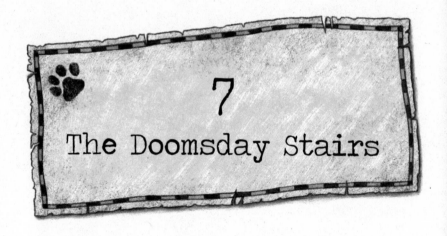

7
The Doomsday Stairs

The Shenanigans started down the Doomsday Stairs.

I stayed put and whimpered.

I knew it was totally teacup of me, but I also knew I'd break my neck goin' down those stairs!

"Come on, boy," Misty said to me.

I whimpered again and took a step back.

This was a grrrave situation!

"You can do it," she said, puttin' on her happy face. "Come on!"

I shook my head and took another step back.

"He can just stay here," Zelda said. "We'll let him out when we get back."

This time my whimper was more like a growl. They couldn't leave me behind!

We squeezed through another passageway and ended up in a small space where an even *narrower* passageway almost U-turned away from us.

"Where does *that* go?" Zelda asked when Misty shone her light into it.

"I have no idea," Misty said.

"I hate this. I feel claustrophobic and cold! And . . . where *are* we?"

"I hate it, too," Misty whispered with a shiver. "And I have no idea."

Out of nowhere a phone started ringing. It was so loud, too, that we all jerked!

And, okay, I admit it—I also yipped.

"Shhh!" Zelda and Misty hissed at me.

The ringing was coming through a small metal grate in the wall. It was right at eye level for me, but the Shenanigans had to squat to see through it.

Once we all had an eyeball in place, Zelda said, "It's the Aunties' office!" It came out in a gush—like she was so relieved to know where she was.

I'd never been inside the Aunties' office, mostly because it was always closed up tight. But now I could

Also, I had to *go*.

"Come on, boy," Misty said, and I could tell she didn't like the idea of ditchin' me. "I'll make sure you don't fall, okay?"

If I had to pick one human on Earth to trust, it would be Misty Nanigan. But I've also got a reputation, all right? My street pack thinks I'm scrappy and smart—a rep that took me years to earn.

And come on. Cawless Crow wasn't gonna peck my eyes out. The stairs couldn't *bite*, or claw me like a cat.

What was I?

Part chicken?

I snorted out a sigh and gave in. I followed Misty in nose-dive position, tryin' not to show that I was shakin' like a Chinese crested on ice.

Zelda took up the rear as we went down and down and down and round and round.

The steps seemed to go on furever! But then suddenly I was plowin' into Misty, and Zelda was rammin' into me.

"What happened?" Zelda asked.

"Dead end," Misty answered.

"Dead end? But . . . why would Mad-Eye Mick build stairs to nowhere?"

Misty moved in a circle, shinin' the head lamp all around. We were crammed on a little platform, sur-

rounded by wood posts and pipes and wires. I was feelin' pretty dark-alley-trapped, too, and then Misty lit up a wide board that ran between two walls, and said, "Maybe that way?"

"Does it *go* somewhere?" Zelda asked.

Misty started along it. "Only one way to find out."

"But . . . are we at ground level?"

"I don't think so," Misty whispered. "I think we'r on the second floor. Between rooms."

"I feel like I'm walking the plank," Zelda mu tered after we'd set off.

The board *was* a little bouncy. But there w walls on both sides of us and no sharky water fall into, and I was so glad to be on all fours that *coulda* been walkin' the plank, for all I cared.

Besides, I know how to swim.

In any case, I stuck close to Misty and walke plank.

We turned and walked another plank.

And another.

Then we went into another nose dive do other set of Doomsday Stairs. The draft was s now, and saltier. *Foggier*.

see that it was a big room, with lots of comfy furniture and a fancy-pants desk with an old-fashioned
phone on it that was ringin' away.

Misty seemed relieved to know where she was,
too, but when the phone kept on ringin', she said,
"Jada's upstairs, but where's Tiana?"

I knew where Tiana was—she was at the market!

I also knew they would never understand me
if I tried to tell them, so I left them spying through
the metal grate and began sniff-snufflin' along the
U-turn corridor, trackin' the draft. And after I'd gone
down it a little ways, my ears perked at the sound of
horns honkin' and tires squealin'. It seemed like there
had to be an opening of some kind down this way.

"Mr. Whiskers?" Misty called. "Mr. Whiskers,
where'd you go?"

I didn't trot back to her because my nose had just
picked up something familiar. Mulchy leaves and
dirt and . . . whoa . . . *me?*

I tracked the smell to a slit in the wall.

No, *three* slits in the wall, two going up/down and
one across. Plus a gap at the bottom.

Well, hot dog! I knew what this was. I could almost not believe it!

I yipped back down the corridor toward the girls, *Mad-Eye Mick built a doggy door!* It was a double-wide . . . pirate-sized . . . *sea* doggy door!

As Misty's head lamp came bobbing along the passageway, I got busy workin' a wooden latch. It was so old that it splintered and fell apart as I nudged it up.

P-oops!

But I was too excited to worry about it. And when Misty and Zelda were close enough, I gave them a happy yippy-yi-yay and head-butted the Sea Doggy Door.

Sure enough, it swung out.

Foggy sunshine streamed in.

"What in the world?" Misty said, clicking off her head lamp.

I pushed through, and when I saw that the Sea Doggy Door was camouflaged by a tall hedge, I did a little prance-dance. My schnoz had been right—I'd smelled my own scent. This narrow space behind the hedge was my shelter—the secret place I go when Auntie Jada shoos me out into the cold. It's got eaves that give some refuge from the rain, and between the house and the hedge there's a soft bed of leaves. Plus a small stash of bones that I've hidden a quick dig away.

My idea of buried treasure!

Especially when my stomach's sounding off with an angry grrrrrowl.

And all this time there'd been a secret door right here?

It was mind-doggling!

"Oh my golly gosh!" Misty said after she and Zelda had crawled out behind me. "A secret way in and out of the house!"

Now, anyone on four paws could tell you this area was my territory because I'd marked it nearly every day since I'd met the Shenanigans. Overkill, I know, and probably a nervous habit, but I've kept it up in case street rrruffians get the bright idea to cozy up to the Merryweather—which they would if they knew how good I have it here.

I'm tellin' you this because the first thing *Zelda* said when she was outside was, "Ew. What is that *smell?*"

I looked the other way, like, *What smell?* But it was a tail tucker fur-sure, and it got me thinkin'— maybe I should cool the tagging.

In any case, Misty was sneakin' a peek through a thin patch in the hedge, saying, "Hey, look! We're near the back door by the kitchen."

"But *now* what?" Zelda said. "None of this is helping us find Dad."

Misty pulled out the card she'd taken from the Henanigan's sweatshirt and showed it to Zelda. "Now we go here."

Zelda read the card. "Treasure Emporium?" She gave Misty a real, uh, *pugnacious* look. "That sketchy place next to Sunshine Bakery on Haight Street?"

"I think so."

"But . . . why?" Zelda turned the card over. "Where'd you even get this?"

Misty squeezed around the hedge, checkin' left and right. "It was next to the . . . the pouch."

"Is that our code name for it?"

Misty pulled off the head lamp and stashed it in the hedge. "Probably a good idea to have one, don't you think?" She started to take off the Goldie Bear beanie, too, but stopped, then pulled it on tight.

"You're really going to wear that?" Zelda asked.

"It's Daddy's," Misty said, her voice crackin' a little.

Then she took a deep breath and started walking.

8
Chewy Louie

Zelda chased after Misty as she hurried along the side of the house, across the grass, and out to the sidewalk. "Why aren't we taking our bikes?" she called.

"Because they're dangerous!" Misty called back as traffic zoomed by on the street. "You know—steep hills and crazy drivers? I almost got *killed* last time, remember?"

"But bikes are so much faster!"

"A faster way to *die*," Misty said. Then she added, "Besides, Mr. Whiskers can't ride a bike."

Zelda trotted along behind her like a coyote on the hunt. "How is *he* going to help us?"

"He found the secret passageway, didn't he?"

Misty said. "And we might still be stuck in that little room if it wasn't for him."

I panted a *Thanks* up at her. She'd stuck up for me like I was *hers*. I liked that. I liked it a lot.

She could tell I was smiling, and tossed me a wink.

So I winked back.

"Whoa!" she said, stopping dead in her tracks. She turned to Zelda. "Did you *see* that?"

"See what?"

"He winked at me!"

Zelda laughed. "Okay. *Now* you're losing it."

But Misty squatted down, held my chops, and looked me right in the eye. "You understand me, don't you, boy?"

I nodded.

"Did you see that?" Misty cried, springin' up. "He nodded!"

Zelda laughed. "No, he didn't. He was just trying to get you to let go of his face."

So Misty looked right at me again and asked again, "Mr. Whiskers, do you understand what I'm saying?" And I was all set to *nod* again, when something bit me. I swear! Something at the back of my neck. A flea? I don't want to say it was a flea, because then you'll think I'm a fleabag or a flea market or a flea-bitten mange magnet or . . .

Well, you get the idea.

But whatever was biting me was sinking its little fangs in deep, and it made me shake my head, then plant myself and scratch.

Misty's face fell, and Zelda started laughin' like a hyena.

Once I'd foiled the fangs, I nodded like a bouncy bobblehead, but it was too late—Misty was already walking on.

Gettin' to the Treasure Emporium *was* a long walk. Especially since Misty took a wrong turn and Zelda got mad and then they marched along like angry ants. Pretty soon we were all hot and thirsty, and since we were goin' a way that wasn't on my regular route, the smells were different and my mental map wasn't much help.

Then *finally* we turned down a street where I caught a familiar whiff—one that put a little spring back in my step.

We were on Chewy Louie turf!

Chewy Louie's an old-school beggar with hind legs so stiff he couldn't outrun a turtle. His eyes are sadder'n a low-slung basset's, so people tend to give him the pity routine when they walk by. It's humiliating, but it keeps him from starvin'. Still, despite the bad hips and the ruff-life stuff, the old boy can be *howlarious*. No one tickles my ribs like Chewy Louie.

It had been a while since I'd been on Chewy's turf, and right now I was feelin' kinda bad about it. Come to think of it, I hadn't seen much of the street pack at all lately because I'd been spendin' so much time at the Merryweather.

So maybe I was a little happier than usual to find Chewy stakin' out a shady storefront corner, belly down on the cool cement, gummin' a fast-food wrapper like it was steak.

"Chewy!" I called with a happy little yip.

Just to set the record straight here, dogs don't need to make *sounds* to talk to each other. We use lots of other ways to communicate—wags and bows and sniffs and eye contact and a bunch of other things. So it wasn't like Chewy and I stood there yippin' and barkin' and growlin' and stuff. We just talked like dogs do, and it went like this:

"Dude!" Chewy said, sittin' up. "Where ya been? Rumor is you split."

Before I could explain, the Shenanigans caught up and Misty said "Come on, boy" as she walked by.

Chewy went a little slack-jawed. "No! For real? You got adopted?"

It was temptin' to puff my chest and make like the girls were mine, but . . . no collar, no tag? I'd be called out and lose all my street cred. "Nah," I said. "I'm just helpin' 'em out. Their dad's been snatched."

"Their *dad* has?"

"Yip. He's a furry fella. Looks like a sheep. Goes by Professor, but his real name's Felix Nanigan."

We had so much to catch up on, but Misty was calling, "Come on, boy! Let's go."

So I got to the point. "Maybe you've seen him?"

"Seen him? Dude, I need more'n that."

I was feelin' dead-ended, but then I remembered—the Henanigan's beanie, which was now stickin' out of one of Misty's pockets.

I ran over to Misty, picked her pocket with a snap of my teeth, and raced the beanie back to Chewy Louie.

"This is his." I dropped it in front of him. "Be quick!"

Chewy took a deep, thoughtful sniff. "Oh, yeah. I know him. He's been by here a few times. Gave me part of his sandwich once." He dived in for another whiff, but by then Misty had stalked over. "Mr. Whiskers! What are you *doing*?"

Chewy gave me a toothy grin. "Mr. Whiskers, huh?"

I wanted to tell him, *Shut up, it's a great name,* but I saved my street cred in the nick of time. "It's long for Whiskey."

His grin drooped. "For real?" he asked, like I was swimmin' in gravy.

Misty leaned over to get the beanie, but real quick I told Chewy, "Don't let her have it," and he snarled like a wildcat.

Misty pulled back. "Bad dog!"

"She thinks I'm a bad dog," Chewy growled my way, but I could tell he was lovin' every bit of this. "It's been a while," he said, low and rumbly.

Misty tried again.

Chewy growled again. He was *really* grinning now, but Misty didn't see it that way. "You want that I share this with the others? Make 'em all take a whiff?"

"You got it," I said back.

Zelda was pulling Misty away. "Just leave it."

"But it's Daddy's!"

"And it's probably got fleas now."

"Doggone it," Misty said with a pout, and I could tell she was mad at me as she pulled me along by the scruff.

"Great to see ya, Chew!" I yowled over my shoulder. "And thanks for the help. We gotta track him down, and quick."

"How do I reach you?" Chewy yowled back. "I'm not much of a sprinter these days, but I can pass word along through Sassy."

Sassy. I hadn't seen her in a while, and I had a sudden pang about it. So I let the truth slip out. "I'm at the Merryweather a lot."

"The Ghost House?"

"Yip! You should hear the chains rattle." Heh-heh.

"Dude!"

"I'll try'n get back here, but meanwhile, get word to Sassy if you can."

"Will do!"

Misty was pullin' me along hard, but I couldn't help askin' Chewy one more thing: "She ever talk about me?"

"She's running with Butch now, so . . . you know."

It felt like a fish bone to the heart. *Butch?* I quit resistin' Misty's tug. Of course Butch. That pedigreedy poacher. I shoulda known.

"That dog was so dirty," Zelda was saying. Then she cut a look at me. "I hope *he* didn't pick up any fleas."

"They sure seemed to know each other, didn't they?" Misty said with a frown.

Zelda just shrugged. "They're *dogs.*"

"Well, that other dog looks like he's had a hard life," Misty said. And as quick as she'd gotten mad at me, she seemed to forgive me. "Do you know him, boy? Who is he?"

I looked up at her, and with all my doggy might I said, *His name's Chewy Louie. He's my friend.*

Part of my street pack.

And yes, he's had a hard life. He's lived most of it on the streets, which I promise you is ruff.

But she didn't understand a word I said.

And it hit me like a ton of sticks—she probably never would.

9
Claw Paws and the Cat

For all the times I'd hung out on Chewy's turf, I'd never even *thought* about going inside the place the Shenanigans called the Treasure Emporium. I mean, why bother? One look through the barred windows told me it was full of rrrrubbish.

That isn't true about the bakery next door, which is chock-full of things worth sittin' pretty for. I've never been above giving a perky look or a friendly wag, or doin' a little prance-dance, to win scraps, and the ones I get from the bakery's sidewalk tables usually come with a nice comment on how cute I am—something a street cruiser like me could use more of.

But it was Sassy who gave me the lowdown on how the bakery's cart of quick-pick breakfast bags gets pulled to the back room after the morning rush. If you wait at the alley door and time it right, you can swipe yourself a doggy bag without anyone in the bakery noticin'. I will warn you, though—the quick-picks always have a muffin inside, and it's a luck-of-the-draw situation. I gave up the gamble a while back because, well, bran.

In any case, when we jangled through the Treasure Emporium door, both Misty and Zelda looked around the place and went, "Wowwwww," like it was full of treasures instead of junk. And while the Shenanigans gawked at junk hangin' on walls and junk sittin' on shelves and junk danglin' from rafters, my nose got to work trying to pick up the Henanigan's scent from the floor. Not an easy thing, considerin' all the other smells. Especially since under it all, lying low and heavy as an old skunk blast, was the hair-raisin' odor of cat.

"Mrow."

My head snapped up.

Drat.

There *was* a cat.

Zelda and Misty looked up, too, and spotted her sitting on a high shelf. Her tail was swishin' sloooow and easy as she watched us.

Never a good sign.

"Oh, how *beautiful*," Zelda said, adjustin' her glasses. "Look how blue the eyes are!"

"And that *fur*," Misty gushed. "It's so fluffy!"

Humans. Sheesh. They're so oblivious. Couldn't they see that right under that fluffy-fur-and-blue-eyes disguise were needle-sharp teeth? Didn't they know that a cat's paws are *weapons*? Ones that shoot out and go straight for blood?

"Mrrrrow," the cat said, this time louder.

"Hey," came a gruff voice from the sales counter. "No dogs in here."

I looked up at the cat and let out a low growl. *Tattletale.*

"He's a therapy dog," Misty rushed to say.

Hot dog! That was some quick thinkin'! I gave Misty an impressed look, but she was too busy bee-linin' up to the counter to catch it.

"Don't give me that bullarky," the man said.

"Where's his vest? Where's his collar? Where's his tag?"

The guy was big, bald, and burly, and his fingernails were long and filed into sharp points, makin' his hands look like big, scary claws.

Between Claw Paws and the cat—who was still watching us, her tail twitchin' like she was just biding her time before she pounced—I was all for hightailin' it out of there. Claw Paws was about to boot me anyway, so why wait around?

But then Misty said, "They give me claustrophobia."

Claw Paws frowned. "The dog wearin' a vest and collar gives *you* claustrophobia?"

"Yes, sir. It's part of my condition." She turned to me. "Isn't it, boy?"

I wagged and gave a little pant. So much for hightailin' it out of there.

"And if you don't mind, sir," Misty was hurrying to say, "we're in a terrible predicament, and we're hoping we can ask you a few questions."

Claw Paws raised an eyebrow at her. "A terrible

predicament, eh?" He looked her over. "How old are you? Nine? Maybe ten?"

"Ten. Yes, sir."

"Well, that's some vocabulary for a ten-year-old." His eyes wandered over to me. "So seein' how you're ten and tossin' around words like 'predicament,' and seein' how you were so easy with that lie about this mutt being a therapy dog, I can't help but feelin' your little 'predicament' involves hustlin' me somehow."

"No, sir!" Misty said. "Really!"

"Well, admit it. That's no therapy dog." He drilled me with a look. "I'll bet he doesn't even know how to sit."

I sat.

Misty and Zelda looked at each other, tryin' to hide their surprise.

"Hmm," Claw Paws said, then commanded, "Down!"

I lay down on my belly.

And that's when I caught a whiff.

The Henanigan had been standing right here!

"We're looking for our father," Zelda said over the counter. "We think he's been kidnapped."

Claw Paws frowned. "You think *I* have your old man?"

"No!" Misty handed over the card. "But this was in his sweatshirt pocket. We think he may have come here asking about some old coins."

I inched back up to sitting, one eye on the twitchy-tailed cat.

"Old coins, eh?" Claw Paws' frown dug in deeper. "Tall guy? Bushy beard? A nail biter?"

"Yes!" Zelda and Misty cried.

Claw Paws' mouth moved side to side.

The cat's tail twitched along.

"Yeah, he was here," Claw Paws finally said.

I snorted. I coulda told them that!

"When?" Misty asked, stretchin' forward like a hound on a leash.

"Let's see . . . ," Claw Paws said, studyin' the ceiling. "That was three days ago."

"And . . . ?"

"And he wanted me to authenticate some old coins."

"What does that mean, exactly?" Misty asked, still strainin' her leash.

"He wanted to know if they were real or fake. Said he was askin' for a friend." Claw Paws snorted. "Like I haven't heard that one before? I'm pretty sure he came in thinkin' they were fakes."

"And . . . ?" Misty asked.

"And I told him I thought they were legit. And seein' how he's gone missing and you're askin' about old coins, I'm guessin' I was right."

"So . . . they're worth a lot?" Zelda asked.

Claw Paws nodded. "That would be my guess."

"How much?" Zelda asked.

Claw Paws shrugged. "I know the sign out front says we deal in rare coins, but . . . it's more old silver dollar stuff, if you get my meaning. What he had was way outta my league."

"So maybe they're not real?" Misty said.

Claw Paws cocked an eyebrow. "And maybe your old man's not missing?"

"If they are real, what would you guess they're worth?" Zelda pressed. "A thousand dollars? Two?"

"Oh, way more'n that. He had a coin from 1778! If

that lot's legit, it may be worth a quarter mil? Maybe more? Like I said, outta my league."

The Shenanigans' mouths popped open like hungry baby birds'.

Zelda was the first to snap hers closed. "So . . . he just left after that?" she asked.

"I told him to go to Christie's auction house, but he didn't want to go downtown with them."

"Why not?" Misty asked.

"Me tellin' him they might be worth a bundle seemed to spook him. He said something about storing them somewhere safe."

I checked on the cat.

She was gone!

I must have some Rhodesian ridgeback in me, 'cause the hairs down my spine went all prickly. How'd I let her ditch me? This was *not* good. I was trapped in this Junk Emporium at a total disadvantage. Cats are stealthy. They can pad around a place or drop down from high shelves, all without a sound. They also know how to climb straight up things. They can *levitate.* How was I supposed to concentrate on what Claw Paws was saying, when lurkin' somewhere behind me was a silent, levitating cat with needle-sharp teeth and weaponized paws?

I wanted out of this junk joint.

I wanted out *bad.*

Misty noticed me twitchin' and gave me a stern look. So I tried to act cool, but it wasn't easy!

Claw Paws was saying, "What I don't get is why you two are here instead of the cops. Not that I *want* the cops showin' up, but if your old man's really gone missing, and you think it's on account of the coins . . . well, sounds like it's time to talk to them, not me."

"It's complicated," Zelda said.

Claw Paws snorted. "Isn't it always."

"Look," Misty said, "before we go, is there *any-thing* else you can tell us? Anything else he said?"

Claw Paws scratched a hand up the side of his neck, flickin' the tips of his fingers out a little when he reached his jaw, then going back to the bottom and flickin' up again. I could tell he was thinking, but it was still a weird thing for a human to do. And *backward.* Who scratches *up*?

Behind me, the cat hissed under her breath.

I whipped around to face her, givin' away how terrified I was of her.

She smiled down at me from a shelf.

Her tail twitched.

She flicked an eyebrow.

I hate it when cats laugh at me.

Misty whispered, "Whiskey, sit!"

So I did. Mostly out of shock. She'd never called me Whiskey before, and she'd sure never told me to sit.

"He did mumble something about this makin' some people really happy," Claw Paws said. "He also gave me fifty bucks for my trouble, so I was pretty happy myself."

"Fifty bucks!" Misty said like she was hackin' up a fur ball. "We only get five for allowance, and we do a lot more than tell someone to go somewhere else!"

Zelda elbowed her. "Was anyone else around when you were talking about the coins?" she asked. "Could someone have overheard?"

"There were two other customers in the shop at

the time, but they were up by that deep-sea diving suit in the front window, so I doubt they could've overheard." He frowned. "Although I might've got a little excited when I saw the 1778."

"What did those customers look like?" Zelda asked, diggin' like a terrier for answers.

"It was a young couple. A man and a woman," he said. "I remember 'cause they spent so much time up there I thought I might finally unload that thing. But they turned out to be lookie-loos." He nodded up at a big, curved mirror mounted on the wall. "I can see pretty much everything from here."

"Did you notice *anything* else?" Zelda asked.

The front door jangled. Claw Paws called out, "Welcome to Treasure Emporium! Let me know if I can be of any help!"

Behind me, the cat hissed again, this time louder.

"Oh, knock it off, Maisy," Claw Paws said to her. Then he looked at me and smiled. "He's been a very good boy."

Well, I guess me being there had been driving Miss Maisy crazy, 'cause instead of calming her

down, that one little compliment sent her flyin'
through the air, hair straight up, weapons out, dive-
bombin' me with a war cry, "Rrrrrrooooooow!"

And maybe I shoulda stood my ground and
fought, but that's not my style, okay? So please don't
call me gutless when I tell you that what I did instead was *run.*

I went up one aisle and around another while the
cat flew after me, levitating over things, weapons

out, *screeching*. I ducked and dodged and weaved and jumped, tearin' around the junk joint until I found myself in a corner of the front window, behind the deep-sea diving suit.

"Mr. Whiskers!" Misty was calling. "Here, boy!"

The cat levitated to the top of the deep-sea helmet and smirked at me.

"Here, pup, pup, pup, pup, pup," Claw Paws called. Like I was a cat!

Flick, flick went Crazy Maisy's tail.

And then, as if I wasn't petrified enough, she licked her lips.

"Mr. Whiskers!" Misty called again. Her voice was getting louder, which was a big relief. "Come on out, boy! It's safe."

Like kibble it is!

I was right, too, 'cause the next thing I knew, that flyin' feline pounced!

I charged out of hiding. My tail knocked something over—of course—but I managed to shoot right into Misty's arms.

Claw Paws scooped up the cat. "You see why I said 'no dogs'?"

After the fur had settled a bit, Zelda knelt by the deep-sea suit and picked up a dripping paper cup off the floor. "Look," she said, holdin' out the cup for Misty to see. "Goldie Bear."

Sure enough, the cup was stamped with the same cartoon bear that was on the Henanigan's beanie. My nose went into action: Coffee. Sugar. Cream turned sour.

"Entitled uni kids," Claw Paws grumbled, taking it from her.

My neck prickled. Uni kids? Maybe from the university where the Henanigan taught?

I squirmed free and sniffed down the area around the scuba suit. I didn't know what to map, so I mapped as much as I could, as fast as I could.

"Really, girls, you need to go," Claw Paws said, holdin' back his hissy cat.

Zelda grabbed me by the scruff. "Sorry," she said. "And thank you!"

Then she hustled me outside.

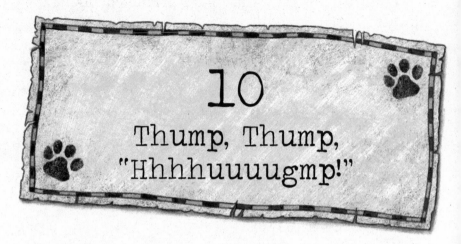

10
Thump, Thump, "Hhhhuuuugmp!"

The Shenanigans were tired, and as snappy as York-ies, by the time we'd walked back to the Merry-weather. I was tired, too, and more than ready to lap up the other half of the bowl.

Yeah, yeah, I know.

Like I said, don't judge.

The back screen door was closed but not latched, as usual. And the door was partly open, as usual. So I could have nosed my way in, as usual, but Zelda held me back. "He has to stay out," she said. Then she gave Misty a hard look and added, "And next time we're taking bikes."

Misty's face scrunched up. Her fists went tight. Her nose flared wide. "Why?" she asked, digging in.

"Because they're way faster."

"No! Why can't he come inside?"

I gave her a grateful pant. She wasn't holdin' her ground about the bike. She was sticking up for *me*.

Zelda dropped her voice. "Because we've got to talk to the Aunties about Dad, and we don't want him setting them off."

I let my tongue hang low and limp and gave them my most pitiful look.

"We at least have to get him some water," Misty said.

I added a pitiful wag to my most pitiful look and turned it on Zelda.

"Okay," Zelda said. "I'll bring a dish out."

"Remember," Misty whispered, "we're not going to tell the Aunties about the secret room."

"I know, but what *are* we going to say?" Zelda whispered back. "I mean, how do we know Dad was trying to sell coins? And where did the coins come from? How did we know to go to the Treasure Emporium?"

Right then the screen door pushed open, and Tiana gave us the hawk eye. "What's all the whispering about?"

The Shenanigans gave Tiana the same look I'd given Tiana one morning when she'd caught me swiping a stick of butter off the breakfast counter. But Tiana was already on to her next question: "Have you girls seen Jada?"

"Uh," Misty said, lookin' to Zelda for help.

"Uh," Zelda said, lookin' back at Misty.

I looked at them both. They were terrible liars! They'd never make off with butter at this rate!

But again Tiana didn't seem to notice. "It's very strange," she said. "I went to the market to get supplies for supper, and when I returned, the front door was wide open and she was nowhere to be found. And she's not answering her phone."

I perked at that. If the front door was open, Rat Man and Poodle Puff had probably skedaddled.

"Well," Misty said, nudging her way inside, "maybe the people who took our dad took her, too."

"What?" Tiana cried. "Why would they want to—"

"You have to tell the police," Zelda said, following Misty inside. "Tell them the guy who took our dad was *fake* FBI. Tell them he's definitely been kidnapped!"

"But . . . Jada said she saw the badge. She said it looked real!"

"So why hasn't Dad called?" Zelda asked. "And where's Auntie Jada?"

"You don't think they're *connected,* do you?" Tiana gasped.

"Sorry, Auntie," Misty said, scooting past her, "but Mr. Whiskers has to come in. Just for a minute. He needs some water."

"But . . ."

I trailed behind Misty like a good little duckling, but when Zelda and Tiana followed Misty to the kitchen to get me some water, I made a break for it. If my hunch was right, either Jada had been kidnapped by Rat Man and Poodle Puff and was nowhere near the Merryweather, or she was in the last place we'd seen her and maybe still had company.

I made tracks through the house as fast as I could, then I dashed up the stairs. "Mr. Whiskers?" I heard Misty call when I'd reached the second-floor landing. "Mr. Whiskers? Where'd you go?"

I kept moving, and when I reached the third floor, I hid in the shadows of an old side table at the end of the hallway. I'm pretty good at hidin' in shadows. Usually it's in alleyways, not carpeted hallways, but the idea's the same. Find cover. Crouch. Ears up. Mouth closed.

In any case, while I was lyin' low by the old side table, ears up, mouth closed, I heard something.

A little thump.

A muffled *"Hhhhugmp!"*

Hmm.

I trotted to the Nanigans' door and put an ear to it.

Thump!

"Hhhhugmp!"

Yip. It was definitely coming from inside.

Now, I may have useless dewclaws instead of thumbs, but . . .

Look, don't spread this around, okay? I don't want to get accused of stuff I didn't actually do, or get latched or locked out of places for good because someone's gotten yappy. What I'm about to tell you is between you and me. Deal?

Okay.

The truth is, I know how to turn a knob.

If I can reach it.

And if it's unlocked.

Also, if the door opens *in*, it's a lot easier than if it opens *out.*

So, yeah. I know how to, uh, *open* and enter. It's not *breaking* and entering because nothing gets broken.

Well, unless my tail gets involved, but never mind about that.

In any case, when my ear picked up another *thump*, "*Hhhhugmp!*" I decided it was time to two-paw the Nanigans' doorknob. It was old and low, and lo and behold, it opened.

Thump, thump, "Hhhhuuuugmp!"

The sounds were louder now, but I couldn't make out what they meant. And I didn't know if either Rat Man or Poodle Puff was still here. So instead of chargin' right in, I crept in. And when I turned the corner . . .

Shiverin' shih tzu!

Jada was strapped to a wooden chair with a belt, her ankles were zip-tied to the legs of the chair, her hands were zip-tied behind her back, and her mouth was stuffed with a sock.

I checked around quick—no one else seemed to be there, but the place looked like my tail had been part of a wild raccoon chase. It was wrrrecked!

I raced over to Jada, planted my front paws on her lap, bit the end of the sock, and tugged it out of her mouth.

"Oh, Whiskey!" she cried, and tears popped from her eyes. "I am so happy to see you! Are the girls coming? Where are they?"

I stretched up to lick her tears and tried to bark out an answer, but she was squirmin' hard to break free and wasn't reading me. And since I know how awful bein' trapped and muzzled can feel, I gave up tryin' to assure her and got to work on freeing her hands.

Not to brag or anything, but I'm a nip 'n' gnaw expert. And since the zip tie around Jada's wrists was nothing compared with a rope or a leash, I peeled back my lips and got down to business.

"That tickles!" Jada cried.

They don't call me Mr. Whiskers for nothing! Heh-heh.

I kept on nippin', and just as her hands snapped free, Misty and Zelda came scurryin' in on a gust of whispers.

They stopped dead in their tracks. "Mr. Whiskers?" Misty gasped. "How did you—"

"Auntie Jada?" Zelda cried, beelinin' toward us. "You're tied up?"

"Oh, girls!" Jada said, rubbing her wrists. "Where on earth have you been?"

Misty and Zelda looked at each other like they were holdin' butter.

"Uh . . . ," Zelda said.

"Walking around town?" Misty said.

My eyebrow twitched at Misty. She'd just pulled a truth-and-dodge—imprrrressive!

Then, while Zelda hurried to take off the belt around Jada, Misty grabbed some scissors and pulled a subject switcheroo. "Why was the front door wide open?" she asked Jada as she cut the ties around her ankles.

"They left in a big hurry," Jada said, freeing one leg.

Zelda started to say, "Those fake—" but Misty cut in, "Who did? And why are you even in our apartment?"

"Cops! They had a search warrant! And badges!" Jada said. "But they weren't actually cops!"

"So . . . what did they look like?" Zelda asked, playing dumb.

"Like cops!" Jada snapped. "Once I caught on, I took pictures of them, but they grabbed my phone and tied me up." She stood. "What do you know about some old gold coins your father has?"

It was Misty's turn to play dumb. "Gold coins?"

"Yes, gold coins. They tore the place apart looking for them."

Misty and Zelda had a very heated but silent conversation while Jada was lookin' away, and finally Zelda told Jada, "He never mentioned any coins."

Wow. Another truth-and-dodge!

"Well," Jada said, "I'm afraid . . ." But then her voice trailed off and her eyes went shifty.

"You're afraid what?" Misty demanded.

"That your father really is in some deep . . . in some big trouble."

"No kidding!" Zelda cried. "He's been *kidnapped*. And now you've been tied up and our apartment has been ransacked! We need to call the police!"

"Right. Right," Jada said, but there was something off about the way she said it.

Something *foxy*.

I wasn't the only one who caught that. Misty zeroed in like a pointer huntin' quail. "You *did* call them before, right? And *they* said they couldn't get involved, right?"

"Of course!" Jada said, but I could smell the lie in it.

So could Misty. "Auntie Jada! What is going on?"

"Never mind, child. Never mind." Jada hurried toward the apartment door. "Just stay here. Just stay here and don't let anyone in. I'm going to talk to Tiana right now, and we'll figure this out. We'll figure it all out!"

When the door slammed closed, Zelda turned to Misty. "What are we supposed to do now?"

Misty frowned. "Well, I'm not going to just sit around here waiting!"

"What else *can* we do?" Zelda asked.

Misty pulled the skeleton key out of her pocket.

She gave her sister a waggish smile.

I knew what that meant, and so did Zelda.

Time to spy!

11
Eye Spy

Zelda grabbed two flashlights; Misty unlocked the secret room. And after a short showdown about me coming along, the three of us were on our way. We pushed past the black flag, kept one eye on Cawless Crow, and started down, down, down the Doomsday Stairs to the planks below.

Maybe it was the extra light from two flashlights instead of one head lamp, or maybe it was because I hadn't killed myself on them the first time, but the stairs seemed easier now.

Misty moved down them fast, chatterin' like a squirrel. "I've been thinking . . . what if Mad-Eye Mick used these passageways to keep an eye on what was going on *inside* the house?"

"Keep a *mad* eye on what was going on, you mean," Zelda said with a snicker as she nudged onto the first landing beside me.

"And if he *did,*" Misty said, steppin' onto the plank between walls, "what if there's a spying port for every room in the house?"

"A spying port? You mean a porthole? Like a *peephole*?" Zelda asked. "That would be more than a little creepy."

"You're right! But maybe he was worried about a mutiny!"

"A mutiny? This is a *house,* not a ship!"

"Mutinies can happen anywhere, can't they? And him being on the high seas for so long with a crew of roguish sea dogs—"

Zelda laughed. "You sound like the Aunties!"

"Well, think about it!" Misty whispered. "Maybe all the time he spent being a pirate made him . . ."

"Paranoid?"

"Yes! Maybe he was worried that any minute someone might stab him in the back, or slit his throat, or *poison* him!"

"In his own house?" Zelda said.

Misty just kept chattering as she scanned the walls with her flashlight. "And even if there aren't portholes—"

"Peepholes."

"Stop calling them that!"

"Well, it's what they would *be,* and I bet a hundred bucks that you were about to say we could *make* them."

I could feel Misty go hot. "You don't have a hundred bucks, and that's *not* what I was going to say. What I was going to say was I bet we could *hear* stuff. Like by holding a drinking glass up to the wall, or with one of those doctor heart-scope thingies."

"We are *not* putting a water glass or a stethoscope up to Ms. LeTrist's room. Or Mr. Bunker's. Or even the empty rooms. We're just not!"

"I didn't say we were!" Misty snapped. "What I care about is finding out what the Aunties are hiding from us. Because they're hiding *something.*" She turned to face Zelda. "I'm not sure they even called the police. You caught that, right?"

Zelda nodded.

"So *why?*"

"I have no idea."

We'd zigged and zagged our way to the second set of stairs, and Misty seemed disappointed that she hadn't found any portholes or peepholes.

"Not everybody wants to be a spy, you know," Zelda said. "Mad-Eye probably just used this as a secret passageway."

"If you ask me, a pirate with a secret room that has a periscope *is* a spy."

When we reached the bottom floor, the Shenanigans went straight to the office grate. Without a sound, they dropped to their knees, bent over, and looked through the grate together.

"They're in there!" Zelda whispered.

I could hear Jada's and Tiana's voices drift through the grate, so I wiggled an eyeball in between the girls to see what was goin' on.

"We can't!" Jada was saying. "Because it won't be just a phone call. Even if we go to the station, they'll want to come here—to the scene of the crime. What if they take a good look around? Ask questions? What if they want to see permits?"

"But we have to!" Tiana said. "Those people who

tied you up said they were going to squeeze it out of him! What if they squeeze the *life* out of him trying?"

Jada rubbed her wrists where the zip ties had been while she paced the room. "Or what if they can't squeeze it out of him and come back to squeeze it out of *us*?" She stopped suddenly. "What on earth has he gotten himself into?"

"Jada, we have to call the police. We owe it to the girls. We owe it to *Felix*."

"Even if it means losing everything?"

Tiana sighed like a tired Bernese settlin' down for the night. "We're on the verge of losing everything anyway."

Jada shook her head. "I know we've got to call, but the thought of losing the Merryweather . . . ?"

Zelda and Misty looked at each other like they'd been goosed. "Oh no!" Misty mouthed, then went back to spyin' through the grate.

Jada was pacing again. "If only we could figure out where they took him! Then the cops wouldn't have to nose around *here*."

"It's a big city, Jada. And what you overheard doesn't give us much to go on. 'It's the weekend, no one will be there'? That could be most anywhere. 'It's not like he doesn't know where he is'? That could be any number of places. And 'Jason took him up the back stairs'? That only eliminates one-story buildings."

"But it tells us the kidnapper's name is Jason!"

Tiana sighed. "It's not enough to go on. We *have* to call the police. And I think we should get the girls down here."

"They didn't seem to know anything about anything," Jada said.

"They're clever," Tiana replied. "I've seen them pull the wool over your eyes many times."

"Over *my* eyes? You're one to talk! Whiskey practically lives here because you're such a pushover!"

Tiana laughed. "We've both got our soft spots. The point is, I can tell when they're lying; you can't."

"Well, the girls are safe upstairs in their quarters. I told them to keep the door locked and stay put. Whiskey's with them, which I'm okay with this once. He'll sound the alarm if something happens." Jada sighed and added, "He pulled that sock out of my mouth. I can't tell you what a relief that was."

Misty and Zelda both looked at me with moon eyes. I gave them a proud pant and a little wiggle in return.

It's nice to be appreciated.

"I'd still feel better about it if they stayed down here with us," Tiana said. "Besides, I think it's time we had a family meeting. I want to look those girls in the eye and find out what they know."

Misty put a finger up to her lips, then tiptoed away from the grate and around the corner to the U-turn passageway.

Zelda followed. "Where are we going?" she whispered.

Misty was moving fast. "Do you want to go back upstairs and have Tiana squeeze *us*?"

"No. . . ."

"So let's go to the police ourselves."

"And tell them *what*?"

"Maybe everything!" We'd reached the Sea Doggy

Door, and Misty was already divin' through it. "We'll figure it out on the way."

But as soon as we were outside, my ears perked at a familiar sound. Zelda heard it, too. "That's Dad's ringtone!" she gasped. "Where's it coming from?"

I knew exactly where it was coming from!

So I yipped at them to follow me, ran around the hedge, and raced toward the back walkway. And I would have led them straight to the kitchen drawer, but what I saw waitin' at the back door made me skid to a stop.

This was not good.

Not good at all.

12
Tour of Terror

It was Butch and Sassy, doing a little spying of their own. Their muzzles were up against the screen door, and they were having a little chitchat about nosing and entering.

"What's the worst that can happen?" Butch was saying.

Butch is a pretty boy. A *pedigree.* One with a collar and tags. His ears and tail have been cropped, and I think his brain was, too. He may be a sharp-lookin' Doberman, but he's more a *Dope*rman, if you ask me. One that's definitely not workin' with a full box of biscuits.

But he's got long legs and a smooth, shiny coat, and acts like he owns the place anywhere he goes.

He brags about his digs up on Nob Hill and about gettin' steak for dinner every night. But even with all he's got, he always takes more'n his fair share of scrounged snacks when he's bummin' with us scrappers.

Worst of all, though?

Even a smart lass like Sass can't seem to resist him.

Grrrrrates my nerves, boy.

So seein' him with Sassy at the Merryweather's back door made me instantly mad at myself for havin' spilled my digs to Chewy Louie. But it *was* good to see Sassy. *Real* good, I realized, now that I'd laid eyes on her. She's more my size than Butch's, with long hair shooting up from the tips of her always-perky ears—something *I* think is, well . . . adorable.

"Sassy," I said, yippin' out her name.

"Sugarpaws!" she said, spinnin' around.

Sassy calls everyone sugarpaws. Or honeypaws. Or, if you're lucky, sweet scruff. And she *does* have a serious sweet tooth. I once saw her hold her own against a wannabe rottweiler over a crème-filled maple bar outside a doughnut shop. It's really not a good idea to come between Sassy and her sweets.

So even though she calls all the boys something sugary, I tried to take the "sugarpaws" as a compliment, instead of lettin' it make me feel like a nicked-up day-old in her barker's dozen variety pack.

Which it could have.

If I'd thought about it more.

"Nice digs, dawg!" Butch said, cuttin' between me and Sassy. "How'd a scrapper like you land a gig like this?"

Misty and Zelda were there now, and the Henanigan's phone was still ringin'. "Where'd these two come from?" Misty asked, givin' Sassy and Butch a worried look.

Zelda swept the screen door open, pointed a stern finger at the pack of us, and said, "Stay."

"We'll be back," Misty assured me, but she kept a wary eye on Butch and Sassy as she disappeared inside.

As much as I wanted to see Sassy, I needed to get rid of Butch, which meant gettin' rid of Sassy, too.

"Look, sorry," I told her. "It was nice of you to come by, but we're in the middle of—"

As usual, Butch cut in. "It wasn't hard to find you once we got close." He hitched his nose toward the hedge. "You staked it out good, dawg." His mouth dropped into a laughing pant. "Nervous of competition?"

Okay, yeah. I hadn't missed Butch at all. "Ya gotta go," I told him.

"Why?" he said, droppin' into another grin. "Think they'll dig me more'n you?"

"Look—" I said, but once again Butch cut in.

"Dawg, word is they named you Whiskey? That's *wild.*"

I'd had enough. "It's Mr. Whiskers to you, *dawg,* and I got more important things to do than chew the fat right now. We're in the middle of trackin' down dadnappers and—"

"We know, sugar!" Sassy said, steppin' closer to me. "It's why we're here."

"It is?" I'm afraid my eyes went instantly sappy looking into hers. She's got lashes for miles.

"Yeah," Butch said, edgin' between Sassy and me. "Chewy filled us in. Had us take a good sniff of that woolly cap."

"And I *do* know your man," Sassy said, shoulderin' Butch aside.

"You do?" I asked, soundin' sharp as slobber.

"We were scouting out the fish market across from the park—" Butch said.

And that's when Sassy did something that surprised Butch *and* me.

She nipped him.

His head whipped her way, teeth showin', but she bared her teeth right back at him and said, "If you don't mind? I was setting the stage?" and just like that, Butch backed down.

I couldn't help prancing in place. What a grrrl!

Sassy turned back to me, cool as a breeze. "Your man takes his lunch in the park, always sits all by his lonesome at the same bench. At first I saw him as just an easy mark, but he's a love, and always willing to share a little something from his backpack. He introduced me to peanut butter with celery. Love, love, love it."

"She likes weird things," Butch said with a sharky grin, tryin' to get back his alpha vibe after being checked by someone half his size.

"So I've noticed," I said, givin' him a steady stare.

It was like a Frisbee flyin' right over his head.

Tiana's voice floated through the screen door.

"Quick," I said to Sassy. "Tell me what you know. I'm runnin' out of time!"

Thankfully, she got down to business. "I was crossing over to the fish market—the one across the street from the corn vendor at the park. You remember, right? We've been there."

I did.

We had.

And I'd gone back many times, hopin' to see her, because . . . well, how could a fella forget a gal who'd taught him the wonders of corn on the cob? Juicy, buttery, roasty but almost fruity, with something to chew on after.

"The street was clear," she was saying, "so I stepped out. But then a car came squealing around the corner. It swerved to miss me, and as it went by, I saw your man looking out the back window at me. He looked terrified, so I chased after the car awhile to let him know I was okay—"

"She was just hoping to score some peanut butter, is the actual truth of it," Butch said.

"Stop it!" Sassy snapped.

"Please," I begged. "Where did the car go?"

Butch huffed. "Look, it's easy. From the fish market, ya go five hydrants, then turn—ow!"

Sassy had nipped him again, and *hard*. And this time Butch kept his teeth bared. "The mutt's in a hurry," he growled. "Make it to the point, already."

Before Sassy could take him on, I asked, "Which way did the car turn?"

Butch kept his eye on Sassy but lifted a front paw for me.

It was his *right* front paw, and something told me Butch couldn't *say* that because he hadn't had to learn his left from right yet.

The pretty boy.

"Thanks," I said. And as I hurried past them, I added, "Hope to see you around sometime, Sassy," before nudgin' my way inside the Merryweather.

But the next thing I knew, they were inside, too! "Get out," I growled. If the Aunties saw them, it would mean a latch on the door fur-sure.

Just then Tiana spotted me. She was in the kitchen, fillin' the teakettle with water. "Whiskey?"

she said to me, then she called, "Jada?" over my head. "Do you have the girls? I'll put Whiskey out and be there in a minute."

And then two things happened at the same time.

Tiana spotted Butch . . .

And I spotted the Shenanigans.

The girls were peekin' out from behind the refrigerator, and when Misty saw me see her, she popped out farther and shook her head, tellin' me not to give them away.

Like I would?

Instead I grinned at Butch and said, "Catch me if you can, rat sniffer!" and tore off through the house, leading Tiana away from the kitchen so the Shenanigans could beat it out the back door.

Sassy didn't join in, and I caught her eye a couple of times as I zigzagged in and out of the rooms downstairs, pretendin' to be terrified while Butch barked and slobbered after me.

Tiana started yelling at Butch, "Leave him alone! Out, you brute! Out!"

I kept weavin' and dodgin' until I saw the girls

slip out the back door. Once they were gone, I made another round of the place to give them time to get away, but when I saw Jada comin' down the stairs faster'n I thought she could, I knew my tour of terror had come to an end.

Time to hightail it out of there!

13
Superior Slobber

Sassy waited for Butch, so I turned tail on both of them and ran after the Shenanigans.

I found them at the back of the property by the toolshed.

Rats.

This meant bikes.

But the shed wasn't open yet, and at the moment the girls were hunched over the Henanigan's phone.

The phone *I'd* rescued!

"Why's it all *slimy*?" Zelda was saying.

Still?

Well, okay, I do make superior slobber.

Misty dropped to her knees when she saw me run up, and hugged me. "You saved us in there!"

Zelda cut the hug short. "Why were the Aunties hiding Dad's phone from us?"

I shook my head. Did a little prance. Tried to drool. *They weren't hiding it,* I yowled, *I brought it home.*

Zelda wasn't paying attention. She was poking at the phone, jabbing harder and harder. "And why did he change his password?"

"Because he's in something deep and doesn't want us to know about it," Misty said.

"But why did the *Aunties* have his phone? And why is it covered in *slime*?"

I yipped.

Stepped forward.

Turned my muzzle to the side, proudly presenting the long stream of superior slobber that was now danglin' from my chops.

Zelda said, "Shh!" but Misty tilted her head a little as she studied me. "Oh my golly gosh," she whispered, then pinched at the stream and stretched it out. "Did *you* find Daddy's phone?"

I yipped, *Yes! Yes! Yes!*

I tell you, that girl is sharp!

"Shh!" Zelda hissed, but Misty asked, "Do you know where he is?"

"Aarf! Aarf! Aarf!"

Okay, I was exaggeratin'. But I *did* know to go five hydrants down from the fish market and hang a right. That was something! A start!

"Aarf! Aarf! Aarf!"

Zelda stopped jabbing at the phone and handed it to Misty, saying, "Here, you try." Then she turned to me and scolded, "Be quiet or the Aunties will find us!"

She was right to be worried, but who found us were Butch and Sassy.

"Dawg, you tryin' to ditch us?" Butch growled.

"Look," I growled back. "We're in the middle of a life-'n'-deather here."

"So let us help," Sassy offered.

"Sorry," I said, twitchin' a look at Butch. "That's not gonna work."

"So *I'm* the problem?" Butch growled, crankin' up the volume. "A mutt like you calling *me* a problem?"

"Stop that!" Misty said, giving up on the phone and slipping it into her pocket. She stepped toward Butch. "Go home!"

Zelda grabbed Misty and opened the shed door. "We've got to get out of here before the Aunties find us."

"Sorry, Sassy," I said over my shoulder as I followed the Shenanigans to the shed. "Thanks for passin' along the info. It was great to see ya."

But Butch wasn't done reclaimin' alpha. He moved toward me with a long, low growl.

"Stop that!" Misty said, grabbing a shovel from inside the shed and nudging him with it. "Go home!"

Butch didn't back down, though. He bared his teeth.

"Forget him!" Zelda said, clipping on a helmet and pulling her bike out of the shed. "We need to go!"

"I can't just leave Mr. Whiskers here!" Misty cried, jabbing at Butch again. "That dog's twice his size! And mean!"

Tiana's voice floated through the air. "Misty! Zelda! Where are you girls?"

"Please come home!" Jada called, her voice drippin' like superior slobber. "We have news about your dad!"

"They do not!" Zelda whispered. "It's a trap!"

Misty was in and out of the shed with her bike in a flash. It had wide tires, little streamers at the ends of the handlebars, and a small basket up front—much too small for me.

But Misty also had a strange cloth bag with her. One that smelled like . . . wet paper . . . mold . . . pine sap . . . and, like everything in the Merryweather, mice.

There were blocky letters across the twin bags that Zelda read out loud. "*Examiner?* Is that an old newspaper delivery bag?"

Misty parked her bike. "Maybe it was once . . . ," she said. She put her head through a big opening in the middle of it, so that the saddlebags rested on her shoulders with one pouch in front and the other pouch in back. Then she clicked on her helmet and grinned. "But now it's a dog carrier."

"Misty, no!" Zelda wailed. "We can't take him. We have to get to the police station. *Now.*"

"I'm not leaving him here to get chewed up by that big dog!" Misty said. She knelt on the ground, patted the front pouch, and said, "Come on, boy."

She didn't have to ask me twice. I jumped in, and she stood up, snugged things tight, and made a wobbly mount onto her bicycle. "Let's go," she said, pushing off.

"Chicken," Butch snarled after us.

That didn't raise a single hair on me.

I *like* chicken!

What *did* hurt, though, was when he said, "Come on, Sass. Let him be a little rockabye baby. You and me? Let's go to my place and have some *real* fun," and Sassy told him, "Sure thing, sugarpaws."

It wasn't the first time Sassy had put a fang to my heart. But also, bein' in that sack did make me feel like a swaddled baby. And when word got out—which Butch would make sure it did—my hard-earned reputation would go rocka*bye-bye*.

But once we were clear of the Merryweather and rollin' along, I shook off thoughts of Sassy and Butch and my ruined reputation, and got my schnoz back on the case.

Not an easy thing at first, seein' how I was stuck in a pouch like a canine kangaroo. But after I twisted around a little and figured out that my front paws could rest on the handlebars, it felt a lot safer.

"Attaboy," Misty said once I'd gotten the hang of things, and when I glanced back, she was grinning.

"You look ridiculous," Zelda said, but she was grinning, too.

"I'm thinking I should get him goggles," Misty called, and they both laughed.

Another ruff thing about riding instead of bein' on four paws was I was havin' trouble following my mental map. The Shenanigans were pedaling fast and seemed to know just where they were going, but I didn't *want* to go to the police station! I wanted to follow the trail Sassy had told me about and see if maybe I could pick up the Henanigan's scent.

But a few intersections later, while we were waitin' on a light to change, I finally caught a whiff. Not of the Henanigan.

Of fish!

Yeah, I know. San Francisco has *lots* of fish, but

under the smell of scales and tails I was catchin' a whiff of something else.

Something buttery delicious.

Something roasty and juicy, with a chew-cob for later.

Yippy-yi-yay!

The gravel in the gravy was that when the traffic light changed, the Shenanigans started rolling the wrong way. "Aarf!" I said, and pushed the handlebars hard to the left.

"Stop that!" Misty barked as we rolled between moving cars toward the middle of the intersection.

Go this way, I barked back.

"What are you *doing*?" Zelda shouted.

"*He's* doing it!" Misty shouted back.

"Well, stop pedaling! Get off!"

"I can't! I'm in the middle of the road!"

Cars swerved to miss us. Horns honked like angry geese. Misty steered and pedaled and jolted us around. And I kept barking, *Go this way! Go this way!*

"Just get to the other side," Zelda shouted, which

was good advice, seein' how we were mostly there now anyway.

As soon as we were safe, Misty got off her bike, onto her knees, and right in my face. "Bad dog!" she cried. "Bad, bad dog!"

"Aarf!" I cried back.

"Were you trying to get us killed?"

"Aarf!" I cried. I worked my way out of the pouch, faced her, and said, *See that fish market? We need to go five hydrants down from there and turn right!*

Zelda had made it across the intersection. "What is the *matter* with him?"

"I don't know," Misty said.

I ran toward the fish market and barked out, *Come on!*

They just stared at me.

So I ran back to them and barked out, *Follow me!*

They just stared at me.

So I gripped the bottom of Misty's pant leg with my teeth and backpawed.

"What are you *doing*?" Misty cried.

"We need to leave him," Zelda said. "Just get on your bike and let's go."

"But . . . I think he's trying to tell us something!"

"Misty," Zelda said in a low growl, "get on your bike and let's go."

"But he did the same thing in the secret room when he found the crow!"

"Misty!" Zelda cried.

So Misty shook me off, stuffed the Kangaroo Pouch in her basket, and got back on her bike.

Follow me! Please! Follow me! I yowled, bounding toward the fish market, then running back to fetch her. *Come on,* I yipped, throwin' my head in the direction of the fish market.

Misty put one foot on a pedal. "He knows something," she said to Zelda.

"Oh, come *on.* He's a *stray.* Misty, he's *wild.* Look at him!"

If I'm tellin' the dog's honest truth, I was *feeling* kinda wild right then. And really furrustrated! How could I get them to follow me?

"The light's green," Zelda said, pushing off in the wrong direction. "Let's go."

Misty followed Zelda into the street, saying, "But . . . what if that goop on Daddy's phone *was* his dog slobber? What if Mr. Whiskers found the phone and brought it home?" She looked over her shoulder at me. "What if he knows where Daddy is?"

I stayed put and yipped my fool head off. *Yes! Yes-yes-yes! Five hydrants past the fish market! Hang a right!*

And then?

I had no idea.

The Shenanigans were halfway across the street now. And even though Misty kept looking back at me, calling, "Come on, boy!" I stayed put. Maybe I'd try to sniff down the Henanigan myself. Besides, there was no way I was gonna go to the police station. Especially not since Zelda had called me a *stray*.

So I'd just given up on howlin' and was strikin' out on my own when I heard Zelda's voice shout, "What are you doing? Come back!"

I turned to see Misty riding toward me. "You go to the police," she called over her shoulder. "I'm going to figure out what he's trying to tell us."

"No!" Zelda screamed. "You can't! We have to stick together!"

"I know my way home," Misty yelled. "Don't worry—I'll be careful!"

I couldn't believe my ears.

"Aaaarooooooo!" I yowled, like a beautiful full moon had just lit up the sky.

"Okay, boy," she said when she reached me. "Lead the way."

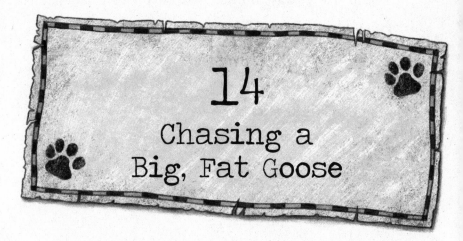

14
Chasing a Big, Fat Goose

Misty and I were zippin' past the fish market when Zelda caught up. "I can't *believe* you're doing this," she yelled.

Misty kept pedaling. I kept running. And dodging and leaping. The sidewalk was an obstacle course of legs and shoes and strollers. There was one chichi Chihuahua that had a lot to say about my ziggin' and zaggin', but I've learned not to listen to chichi Chihuahuas in or out of strollers.

I did toss her a *Yippy-bye-yay, little yapper!* look, which only made her complain louder.

In any case, Zelda's voice cut through my concentration again. "Dad's going to be so mad when he finds out you chose a *dog* over me!"

"I didn't *choose* him," Misty shouted back. "He *knows* something, can't you tell?"

I charged ahead, passing by one . . . two . . . three . . . *four* hydrants, while the Shenanigans rode along in the street next to me, barking at each other the whole way.

Finally, at the fifth hydrant, I turned right, ran for another block, and then . . . slowed down. My nose was in tracker mode, but after another block it still hadn't picked up a trace of the Henanigan.

Doggone it.

Now what?

I didn't know, but I moved forward with my eyes peeled, my ears perked, and my schnoz on full snuffle.

Zelda and Misty were riding alongside me now, and Zelda was gettin' madder with each turn of her pedals. "Where are we going? Why are we following him? This is just a wild goose chase!"

And then an awful thought slapped me upside the schnoz.

What if Butch had played me?

I stopped in my tracks.

That *would* be just his style.

I felt like yowling. Why had I just lapped up everything he'd said?

Five hydrants?

The bug brain probably couldn't even *count* to five!

The Shenanigans had kept going, but now they U-turned and pulled up to where I was standing still, pantin' my fool tongue off. They both stared at me like, *Well?*

I looked away.

"Oh, great," Zelda said. "Just great."

I side-eyed Misty as she studied my hangdog head. "Mr. Whiskers?" she asked.

I couldn't look at her. I just couldn't.

Finally she took a deep breath and told Zelda, "I'm so sorry," which made me feel *really* rotten. She *had* chosen me over Zelda, and I'd let her down.

But then her eyes rose into full moons. "Goldie Bear!" she cried as she pointed to a giant cartoon bear painted on a building down a side street.

"Is that the back of the college stadium?" Zelda asked.

"Yes! So maybe Dad's . . . ?" Misty said, thinkin' out loud. "Do you think he's . . . ?"

The Shenanigans turned to stare at me. I didn't really understand what they were so excited about, but I gave them my best *Yeah, I'm the smartest doggy in the whole wide world* pant anyway, hopin' I'd stumbled onto a secret back door out of the doghouse I was in.

A little gasp came from Zelda, and she said, "Misty, this morning . . . when that guy came for Dad . . . do you remember how Dad was going to go back upstairs, but the guy stopped him?"

"Sure," Misty said.

"And do you remember what he asked Dad?"

Misty nodded. "He asked him if he had his keys."

"Right! Not 'Do you have your ID?' or 'Do you have your wallet?' or 'Do you have your phone?' or any combination, just 'Do you have your keys?'"

Misty blinked at her. "And . . . ?"

"All he cared about was Dad's keys! And then when we were spying on Jada and Tiana in their office, Tiana said that those fake cops who tied Jada up had said—"

"'It's not like he doesn't know where he is,'" Misty rushed to say.

"And 'It's the weekend, no one will be there'!" Zelda said, bouncing a little on her bike seat.

"And that they took him up the back stairs!" Misty cried, bouncing now, too.

They were actin' like they'd landed in a big pile of leaves, but I still had no idea what they'd figured out.

Misty reached over and ruffled me. "You are the smartest doggy in the whole wide world!"

Then Zelda grinned at me and said, "Or maybe just the weirdest. Or luckiest. But whatever, thanks for leading us here, Mr. Whiskers."

Yip, I'd somehow escaped the doghouse! I ran alongside as they pedaled over to the Goldie Bear stadium and got on a bike path.

After we'd gone a short way, Zelda pointed and said, "Let's cut through campus this way!" and rode toward an open gate.

In all my tours of San Francisco, I'd never scouted out the college before. It had always seemed so . . . *pedigree.* A place where a scruffy fella like me would not be welcome. But as I ran along, I wondered *why* I'd thought that. Sure, the place was big, with fancy buildings and tidy lawns and plants and stuff, but the people we were goin' past seemed pretty scruffy themselves. A couple of them had a Frisbee flying. I'm great at Frisbee! And the trash cans we went by looked *very* promising. Also, I was seein' *no* competition, which meant that a prancer like me could score some tasty treats, easy! The farther we went, the more I thought that this would be a really *great* place to cruise around.

Two quick pants after I'd had that thought, a siren chirped behind us. The bike path we were on was next to a road that went between tall buildings, so the chirp couldn't have been for us, but when I looked over my shoulder, I saw that a police car seemed to be tailin' us. And sure, this car had Goldie Bear grinnin' on the side of the door, but believe me, I know a cop car when I see one.

Chirp, it went again, and as the driver's window came purring down, I saw that the cop behind the wheel was lookin' right at me.

I almost choked on superior slobber.

It was Poodle Puff!

The Shenanigans looked over and almost choked, too, because, well, they recognized her, too.

"She's campus police?" Misty gasped.

"Be cool!" Zelda whispered, still pedaling along. "She doesn't know us. We saw her from the secret room and—" She went moon-eyed. "Oh no! She looked at that picture of us! The one on Dad's desk! And Jada said our names!"

Misty's face fell, but she tried to sound convincing when she said, "But that picture's old. From before you got glasses! And we're wearing helmets now, so—"

"So why's she stopping us?" Zelda hissed.

The police car chirped again, and when we all came to a stop, Zelda called, "Yes, Officer?"

Poodle Puff gave us the once-over. "No dogs allowed on campus."

"Oh," Zelda said. "Sorry. We didn't know."

"He's my therapy dog!" Misty said.

"Right," Poodle Puff snorted. Then she barked, "Pick him up and get him out."

"Yes, Officer," Zelda said. She turned to Misty, and under her breath she said, "Just do what she says."

So Misty slipped the Kangaroo Pouch back on over her shoulders, and I hopped into the front part, actin' like the best doggy ever—one that could really be a therapy dog.

Poodle Puff watched the whole time. "What are your names?" she asked like *she'd* caught a whiff of something fishy.

"I'm Lisa!" Zelda rushed to say. "And this is my sister, Sarah. We're sorry we didn't know about the rule. We'll leave right away."

"Your *last* name?" Poodle Puff asked, definitely sniffin' down something.

"Johnson," Zelda said. Then, cool as a breeze, she asked, "What's yours?"

Poodle Puff ignored the question. "What are you doing on campus, anyway?"

"Just exploring," Zelda said. "We live nearby. It's our first time. Sorry we didn't know about the rule."

"Can I see some ID?"

"ID?" Misty asked. "I'm ten! She's eleven. We don't have IDs."

"Do your parents know you're here?"

"Our mom said it was okay," Zelda said. "We don't, y'know, *have* a dad."

"Hmm," Poodle Puff said with a frown. "Well . . . just get that dog off campus. And don't dawdle."

"Okay," Zelda called. "Sorry again!"

The car pulled away, and Misty whispered, "You were amazing!"

"Maybe not amazing enough," Zelda said, looking after the car.

"Do you think she knows?"

Zelda gave a little nod. "I think she might."

"So . . . what do we do?"

"Well, we can't exactly ask campus police for help," Zelda said. "But I'm sure not leaving now. We *must* be on the right track!"

"So . . . get to Daddy's office?"

Zelda nodded. "And get there *fast.*"

15
Blazin' Biscuits!

"In here!" Zelda called, making a quick turn onto a
little plaza in front of a big building. Then she took
an even sharper turn around a stone planter toward
a bike rack.

I was in the Kangaroo Pouch, and Misty almost
dumped us both tryin' to keep up.

"Let's hide the bikes here," Zelda said, skidding
to a stop.

Maybe it was in a corner of the plaza, and maybe
there were stone planters and long cement benches
nearby, but as a place to hide? It was terrible! The
bike rack was nearly empty.

Misty stepped off her bike, knelt, and let me hop

out of the Kangaroo Pouch. Then she grabbed me by the scruff, looked me right in the eye, and said, "Stay. And don't make a sound."

I could sit and pant quietly like a good boy, but if they were gonna *leave* me here? Furrrrgetaboutit!

The whole time the Shenanigans were stashing their bikes, helmets, and the pouch, they were lookin' over their shoulders and hissin' at each other like sneaky snakes.

I shook my head. Someone really needed to teach them how to make off with the butter!

Finally Misty told Zelda, "Okay, fine. You do it."

So Zelda hurried across the plaza to the building's double glass doors, tried to open them, and ran back. "It's locked."

Misty whispered, "Should we check the side doors?"

"Good idea."

They didn't tell me to stay, so I trotted along as they tried every door, all the way around the building.

All of them were locked.

"So now what?" Misty asked when we were back at the bikes.

"Maybe we should split up and wait by doors for someone to come out, then catch the door and sneak in?" Zelda said.

"But they could be torturing Daddy this very minute!"

Suddenly Zelda grabbed Misty's arm. "Quick! Hide!"

I looked across the plaza and . . . blazin' biscuits! It was Poodle Puff.

At first the Shenanigans just crouched by their bikes, but that was like hidin' behind chicken wire. So they followed me on their hands and knees as I sneaky-pawed over to the cement benches.

The benches were low, but solid and long enough to hide all of us. Misty and I took one, while Zelda stayed back at the other. When we poked our noses around the side, we saw that Poodle Puff had just reached the glass doors. She looked over both shoulders, then unlocked the door and pulled one side open.

Before going inside, though, she looked around *again*. And just as her head was turning toward the door, it stopped, then slowly craned back to the bike rack.

Her eyes narrowed.

"Uh-oh," Misty whispered.

I gave her cheek a nose nudge, tellin' her not to worry, but then Poodle Puff spat out a curse—the one humans always use when they step in something one of us furry fellas has left in the grass. But she didn't march over to the bikes. Or look for us behind the planters or the benches or anywhere else. She threw open the door and went inside.

The door began shutting behind her. I could tell it was on an automatic closer—my tail had figured out about those the hard way. So I knew the door would move slowly for a little while, then slam shut.

I waited, hopin' to let Poodle Puff get well inside and still leave enough time to slip through the closing door. If I guessed wrong—if I missed by even a little—I'd be one ugly pup, with maybe a smashed schnoz, or a broken tail, or . . . or worse.

But if I *could* make it inside?

I'd be a hero!

So I waited . . .

And waited . . .

Then I shot out from hiding like a doggy dart!

"No!" Misty cried, but every bit of me was aimed at that door—at the opening getting smaller and smaller and smaller.

When I reached it, I dived through, flipped up my tail, rolled on the floor, and then *whoosh-thwonk,* the door slammed closed.

Made it by a whisker!

I looked through the glass at Zelda and Misty as they raced over to the door. And after giving them a happy pant from inside, I stood on my hind legs, stretched my paws to the door's crossbar opener, and pushed to unlatch it.

Zelda pulled the door open and the Shenanigans scurried inside.

"Oh my golly gosh!" Misty said, hugging me.

Zelda gasped. "That was un-be-lieeeeevable!"

I gave her a happy pant.

Hero! Yip, that's me.

But all of that was forgotten when Misty yanked Zelda against a wall and whispered, "She's down by the elevator."

I peeked around the corner, and there was Poodle Puff, jabbin' her finger at the wall button.

"Come on!" Misty whispered. "Let's take the stairs!"

We sneaky-pawed over to a door that had a zigzaggy-stairs design on it, and Zelda made sure to close it veeeeery quiiiietly once we were through it. Then we raced up the steps, taking them two at a time, until we came to a door on the third floor.

"Let's find a place where we can see Dad's office door," Zelda said, breathing hard. "See if she goes inside it."

"And if she does?" Misty whispered.

"Then we find a phone and call the *real* police!"

Misty nodded. "Good plan."

Zelda opened the door a little to make sure the coast was clear. Then we all stepped out, scurried down the hallway, took a left turn, and ran down another hallway. I could tell they knew exactly where they were goin', but before we got there, we heard a ding.

In a flash Zelda scooped me up and dived for cover around a corner. Two wags later we peeked around it and spied Poodle Puff steppin' out of the elevator. She walked up the hallway toward us but stopped a few doors down and rapped it with her knuckles. *Knock-knock. Knock. . . . Knock-knock. Knock.*

"That's Daddy's office!" Misty breathed.

"Do you think that was a secret knock?" Zelda asked.

Poodle Puff hit the door again. *Knock-knock. Knock. . . . Knock-knock. Knock.*

"That was definitely a secret knock!" Misty agreed.

This time the door opened, but instead of Poodle Puff goin' inside, she yanked a man out into the hallway.

It was Fishy, only without the crooked whiskers.

Poodle Puff pulled the door closed and hauled Fishy our way by his arm.

The Shenanigans held their breath.

I quit panting.

But just when we thought we were caught, Poodle Puff stopped, right down the hallway from us.

She let go of Fishy and said, "Anything?"

Fishy shook his head. "Look, this has gotten way out of control. I don't even think the coins exist!"

"I know what I heard!" Poodle Puff hissed with her nose right in his face. "And I heard it twice! Once when he was on the phone, and once when we followed him to the Treasure Emporium. They're for real and he's got them *somewhere.*"

"Well, he's not talking, and I think we've taken this far enough. I was in it to pay off my debt, not to go to jail!" Fishy took a step back. "Where's your stupid boyfriend, anyway?"

"He's busy, all right? And no one's going to jail." Her frown dug in deeper. "But we do have a problem . . . which I'm thinking may be an opportunity in disguise."

"Really? This again? How many times have you said that to me in my life? When has it *ever* been true?"

"Here's the deal, baby brother," Poodle Puff said, slicking right over his questions. "I think his kids are on campus."

"What?!"

"Calm down, okay? I'm not sure, but I *think*. There was a picture of two girls on the desk in his apartment. These kids sure looked like them."

"I saw his daughters this morning!" Fishy said. "One of them has long, wild hair, the other wears glasses. And they had a dog."

"Well, that's definitely them, then. Dog and all." Poodle Puff snorted. "Clever little liars."

"What do you mean?"

"They said their last name was Johnson and told me they didn't have a dad." She frowned. "Why would they lie to me? They can't know who I am!"

"Maybe it's not them?" Fishy said. "Or maybe they're onto us?"

"How could they be onto us? Unless *you* blew it somehow?"

"Me?! I've been locked up with *him* all day!"

Poodle Puff shook her head. "Whatever. The

point is, they're somewhere nearby. Their bikes are parked right outside the building."

Fishy put his hands up like he was being robbed. "I'm done. I'm gone. I'm out."

"You kidnapped the man," Poodle Puff said, holdin' him back. "You kidnapped him, tied him up, and tortured him."

"You *told* me to! You said he would recognize you, so *I* had to do it!" Fishy looked away. "Besides, I didn't *torture* him. I pinched him a bunch, is all."

"You *pinched* him?"

Fishy shrugged. "You said to squeeze him . . . so I did!"

Poodle Puff rolled her eyes. "Well, no wonder he's not talking!" Then she drilled him with a look. "Still. You're the one who kidnapped him. There's no getting out of that."

Fishy looked at Poodle Puff like he'd been cornered by a snarlin' shepherd. "You have always been like this! You have always just *used* me."

Poodle Puff shrugged. "Look, you'll get as much out of this as we will, so—"

"But if his *kids* are here, they're probably looking for him! Pretty soon they'll get someone to let them in the building!"

"No, they won't. As soon as I'm done here, I'm going to go find them and . . . contain them. And while I'm finding them and *containing* them, you're going to go in there and tell the good professor that we have his kids, and if he wants them back, all he has to do is tell us where the coins are."

"You're blackmailing him with his *kids*? That's what evil overlords do! And I'm not an evil overlord!" Fishy shook his head. "Besides, it's not like you actually have to *have* the kids to tell him that!"

"Hmm," Poodle Puff said. "That's true." She cocked her head a little. "Did you blindfold him like I asked?"

"Yes! I put a pillowcase on his head."

"Well, fine," she said with a little smirk. "You go round up his kids, I'll deal with the professor."

"But—"

"Go! I want to get this over with, and obviously you're not up to the job."

"But—"

"Text me a picture when you've found them," Poodle Puff said, then shoved Fishy back down the hallway. "Now go!"

"I am so done with you," Fishy said, hurrying toward the elevator. "You *are* an evil overlord!"

Poodle Puff laughed. "You'll take that back when this is over and you're rich."

Then she walked down the hall, opened the Henanigan's office door, and disappeared inside.

16
The Evil Overlord

When the coast was clear, Zelda stood up and said, "Let's go find a phone and call the police."

"We don't have time!" Misty said. "Didn't you see her face when she said she'd take care of things? She went in there to torture him! We need to save Daddy. *Now.*"

"But . . . how?"

"There's three of us!" Misty said. "And we know the secret knock!"

"*Three* of us?" Zelda gave me a look.

Misty held her ground. "We wouldn't be in the building . . . or here at *all* if it wasn't for him."

I panted and gave Zelda a look back. *Yip. All true.*

"It'll be easy," Misty said, and then her words started comin' out in a rush. "We go up, we do the secret knock, she thinks it's her brother, she opens the door, and we charge! We *flatten* her, then tie her up."

"You call that easy?"

But before Zelda could stop her, Misty was running down the hall.

Zelda chased after her, trying to talk her out of it, but Misty's knuckles hit the door. *Knock-knock. Knock. . . . Knock-knock. Knock.*

Zelda held her head like it might explode. "This is crazy!"

But it was too late. The door flew open, and Poodle Puff snapped, "I told you to—"

Misty dived in, head-butting her right in the stomach.

"Oof!" Poodle Puff gasped, doubling over.

And just like that, Zelda was all in. She jumped onto Poodle Puff's back and yanked her hair puff with both hands, screaming, "Get down on the floor, you evil overlord!" She yanked harder. "Get down or I'll gouge your eyes out!"

"Wow!" Misty cried. "Awesome!"

I'd like to say that I jumped into the fight, too, but the dog's honest truth is, I didn't.

I *couldn't.*

I'd been stunned stupid by *bones.*

They were everywhere! There were bones in cases, bones on shelves, bones on the desk where the Henanigan was bound to a chair, with a pillowcase over his head. There were small bones, medium bones, large bones . . . and there was one standin' in a corner that was *way* bigger than any bone I'd ever seen.

This was the Henanigan's *office?*

Why hadn't anyone told me he worked in doggy heaven?

So while I stared at bones, Zelda held on tight to Poodle Puff as she bucked like a bronco, and Misty yanked the pillowcase from the Henanigan's head. It wasn't until Zelda got thrown off and her glasses went flyin' that I snapped out of the trance. Because when that happened, Poodle Puff turned the tables, grabbing Zelda by the throat and pinning her against the wall. "Get away from him!" she ordered Misty, who had just worked a fat strip of tape off the Henanigan's mouth. "Get away from him or I squeeze."

Zelda gasped for air.

Misty backed away.

"So, Professor," Poodle Puff said with a smirk. "Where are they?"

"Don't tell her, Dad!" Zelda croaked.

Poodle Puff squeezed.

"Stop!" the Henanigan cried. "Please. Put her down and I'll tell you."

"Tell me, and I'll put her down," Poodle Puff said like she was holdin' all the biscuits.

Too bad for her, there was one biscuit she'd ignored.

Me!

I crouched, then shot through the air and sank my teeth into her backside, and . . . fang-dango! I must have a little pit bull in me, 'cause I locked down hard and wasn't about to let go!

"*OOOOOWWWW*," Poodle Puff screeched at the top of her lungs. She dropped Zelda and a whole

slew of grassy words, but even with me clamped on tight, *she* didn't drop to the ground.

Zelda retrieved her glasses while Misty grabbed the big bone in the corner with both hands. But when Misty cocked the bone back to hit Poodle Puff, the Henanigan cried, "Don't! That's an allosaurus femur from the late Jurassic period!"

"Sorry, Daddy!" Misty said as she swung. "Today it's a bat!"

The swing landed hard, Poodle Puff went down, I let go, and Zelda cheered, "Yes!"

"Girls!" the Henanigan said. "Untape me before she comes to or that other one comes back!"

"There are three of them, Daddy," Misty said.

"Three of them?"

Misty nodded. "Her brother and her boyfriend."

So while Misty was busy unwrapping the tape from around the Henanigan's wrists and ankles, explaining to him what had happened, Zelda snagged the fat roll of tape that was sitting on the desk and got busy wrapping Poodle Puff up. First she did her ankles, then her hands, then a nice long piece across her mouth. "See how *you* like it," she said when she was done.

Then *ping,* a sound came from somewhere around Poodle Puff.

Zelda patted her down and dug up two phones. "I recognize this one," she said. "It's Auntie Jada's!" She slipped it into her pocket, then looked at the other one. "So this one must be hers." She forced one of Poodle Puff's thumbs onto the screen, then took a step back and flicked her own finger against the phone. "There's a text that says, 'I can't find the girls,'" she said.

Misty got all excited. "Text him back! Say, 'That's okay, come to the office. I've got the coins.'"

Zelda blinked. "Brilliant!"

Misty grinned. "Why, thank you!"

So while Zelda's thumbs were flyin', Misty pulled the Henanigan's phone from her pocket and said, "Here's your phone, Daddy. Call the real police."

"How in the world did you find it?" the Henanigan asked. "He tossed it out the window in Golden Gate Park!" His face scrunched up as he took it from her. "What's this sticky stuff all over it?"

I yipped and gave him a happy pant. *Superior slobber at your service!*

So the Henanigan called the real police, and right when he hung up, there was a *Knock-knock. Knock. . . . Knock-knock. Knock* at the door.

"Here we go," Misty whispered.

The Henanigan got in position.

Misty picked up the allosaurus bat.

I bared my teeth, and I swear one fang twinkled.

Knock-knock. Knock. . . . Knock-knock. Knock.

Zelda whooshed open the door.

The Henanigan grabbed Fishy by the shirt and dragged him inside the office.

Zelda slammed the door closed.

I rocked back, ready for action!

But I never got to pounce because Fishy put his hands straight up in the air and said, "I'm sorry! I'm really, really sorry!" Then he noticed Poodle Puff with her mouth taped closed and said, "Oh, thank you! You have no idea. Thank you, thank you!"

"If you're serious," the Henanigan said, "you'll tell us where we can find her boyfriend."

"I'll tell you anything!" Fishy said. "I am so glad

to be caught. What a nightmare. *She's* a nightmare! How did I ever let her strong-arm me into this? What's the *matter* with me?" Then he cringed and said, "Are you okay? Do you want to tie me up? I wouldn't blame you. Go ahead. I'm so sorry."

The Henanigan just stared at him.

Poodle Puff groaned. She was comin' to!

"Okay," Fishy said, backin' away from her. "Well, I'll just sit over here in the corner until you decide what to do with me. Just keep *her* away from me, okay?"

Poodle Puff's eyes opened, and when she understood what had happened, she started squirmin' around on the floor, trying to yell through the tape.

Misty poked her with the bone. "Look, you evil overlord. The real police are on their way, so give it up." She cocked her head my way. "Unless you want us to let him take another bite out of crime?"

Zelda laughed like it was the funniest thing she'd ever heard, and the Henanigan smiled for the first time since we'd barged in. "Girls?" he said, then he scooped them into his arms and buried his furry face in their shoulders.

"Aaarooo!" I yowled from the sidelines, and the next thing I knew, he'd scooped me into the pack.

I did a squirmy dance and tried to lick all of them, and for that one wonderful, waggy moment I felt like part of the family.

And then there was a knock on the door.

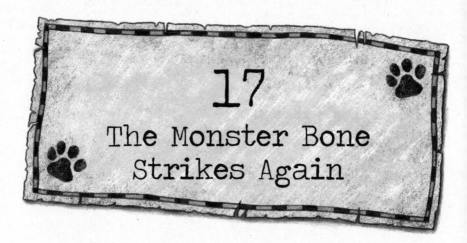

17

The Monster Bone
Strikes Again

Knock-knock. Knock. . . . Knock-knock. Knock.

Everyone went quiet.

Well, everyone but Poodle Puff, who squirmed hard and tried to yell.

Misty threatened her with the Monster Bone, while I got in her face, showed my teeth, and let out a low growl.

She quit squirming.

Knock-knock. Knock. . . . Knock-knock. Knock.

"It's her boyfriend," Fishy whispered from the corner where he was sitting. "He's horrible. Don't let him in!"

Everyone held still, not knowing what to do. Then

Poodle Puff made a screeching noise that I swear came blastin' out her nose and *ears.*

A quick shake later, the office door opened.

All by itself.

Rat Man walked in with keys jinglin', but he stopped in his tracks when he saw Poodle Puff wrapped up on the floor. Then, when he took in Misty with the Monster Bone ready to swing, me flashin' fangs, Zelda itchin' to bronco ride, and the Henanigan free as a bird, he dropped the keys, turned around, and *ran.*

Well, yippy-yi-yay! You run, I chase!

I was through the door and on his tail in a flash, with Zelda and Misty right behind me.

The Henanigan shouted, "No! Come back!"

Instead of takin' the stairs, Rat Man charged for the elevator. And then he just *stood* there, jabbin' the wall button.

Humans can be very confusing. Why ride when you can run? When we caught up to him, Misty didn't mess around. She rammed him hard with the Monster Bone and pinned him against the elevator doors.

Rat Man couldn't reach us, but that didn't stop him from using very grassy language, or trying his darndest to kick me. And even pinned to the doors, he kept reachin' for the wall button.

All of this happened like chasin' a rabbit—zip, zop, zoop. So the Henanigan showin' up just then didn't mean he was *slow*. It just meant that we were *fast*. Good thing, too, because right when he caught up, the elevator went *ding*, and the doors slid open.

Rat Man stumbled backward right into two big cops.

One of the cops had whiskers like a Scottie.

The other? Not a hair in sight.

"I'm the one who made the call!" the Henanigan rushed to say. He pointed to Rat Man. "He's one of the three who kidnapped me."

The policemen looked at the Henanigan's fuzzy face.

They looked at *my* fuzzy face.

Then they looked at the Monster Bone and the Shenanigans.

"Ho-boy," Scottie Cop said. "This is going to be some report."

"Where are the other two perps?" Hairless asked.

"In my office," the Henanigan said. "This way."

But right then a thought seemed to whoosh from Misty to Zelda to me, and we all raced back to the office.

Sure enough, Fishy was in the middle of settin' Poodle Puff free.

"You *faker*," Misty cried, anglin' an angry look at Fishy.

"We *believed* you," Zelda spat out.

I summed things up with "Grrrrrr!"

"She *made* me!" Fishy cried. "You have no idea what it's like!"

"Oh, right," Zelda said. "She was all hog-tied with her mouth taped shut, and she *made* you?"

Poodle Puff finished rippin' the tape from her mouth. "We need to get *out* of here!" she screamed at Fishy. "We kidnapped a professor! Impersonated FBI agents!" She started untapin' her ankles. "Pick up a bone and *fight* them, you idiot!"

"*Hh-hmm*," came a voice from the doorway.

Poodle Puff whipped around, then deflated like a bitten balloon—the real cops were standin' there next to the Henanigan and Rat Man and had heard everything.

Rat Man was handcuffed, and he gave Poodle Puff a glare as Scottie Cop pushed him forward and said, "The three of you—sit there on the floor."

Then the other cop said, "You have the right to remain silent—"

"She doesn't know how," Fishy muttered, while Scottie handcuffed him.

"Anything you say can and will be used against you in a court of law."

"I want a lawyer!" Poodle Puff screamed. "That fleabag *bit* me! Those girls *attacked* me!"

"See?" Fishy said.

The cops were out of handcuffs, so they wrapped Poodle Puff's wrists in tape, and nobody stopped Misty when she slapped some over her mouth and said, "He's Mr. Whiskers to you, you evil overlord!"

Fishy snickered. "What'd I tell you?"

After the cops had finished collarin' the kidnappers, they told the Henanigan that they wanted to take his statement down at the police station.

The Henanigan looked at Misty and Zelda, then back to the cops. "I need to get my girls home."

"We rode bikes, Daddy," Misty said. "We need to get *them* home." She eyed me. "And him."

"We can just meet you at home, Dad," Zelda said. "We're old enough."

The Henanigan took the Monster Bone from Misty and put it aside carefully. Then he said "Give me just a minute" to the cops and led the three of us into the hallway. "You sure you know the way?" he asked.

Misty laughed, "How do you think we got here?" and slipped me a wink.

I slipped one back.

"Please be careful," he said, givin' them each a kiss on the forehead. "And please tell the Aunties that I have . . . *things* I need to discuss with them tonight. Important things."

Zelda frowned. "Okay, but first you're going to discuss them with us."

The Henanigan looked a little surprised.

Zelda dug in. Crossed her arms. "We know everything, Dad."

Misty crossed *her* arms. "And we have some things *we* need to discuss with *you*."

"And that has to happen *before* you talk to the Aunties," Zelda said. "Deal?"

The Henanigan made a long, slow nod. "Fair enough." He turned to go, then turned back. "And, girls? *I* want to know everything. About what you discovered, about how you found me . . . everything."

Misty grinned at him. "We *urned* our way, Daddy."

He broke into the biggest smile I'd ever seen on the Henanigan. "That's my girls!"

Then he went back to the office.

And we headed for the stairs.

18
Gettin' the Story Straight

I didn't want to ride in the Kangaroo Pouch, so when Misty offered, I backed away.

"You want to run all the way home?" Misty asked.

Home?

"Aarf!"

Misty got on her bike. "Well, don't get lost, okay?"

"Aarf! Aarf!" I answered.

"Okay, then . . ." She pushed off. "Let's go."

So I followed along, happy to let them lead the way. We did go past the fish market, and when we went by the corn vendor, I couldn't help lookin' around for Sassy. Not that I was expectin' to see her, but a fella can hope, can't he?

Besides, I really needed to thank her for the tip. After all, she was the reason I'd gotten to be a hero.

But . . . did that mean I had to thank Butch, too?

Gnaw!

So he knew how to count to five. So what? He was still a Snobby Hill soft paw!

But then the thought of Butch and Sassy bein' together crept in, and I shook the whole idea off. *Just furgetabouther,* I told myself, and perked my ears at the Shenanigans, who were gettin' their story straight as they rode along.

Even with all the street noise, it was easy for me to hear them because they were ridin' single file, with Zelda up front, and they were shoutin' everything back and forth.

"So," Misty was saying, "when we get home, we tell the Aunties that Daddy's okay, that the kidnappers are arrested, and that Daddy wants to talk to them when he gets home."

"And," Zelda said, "we tell *Dad* that he has to tell the Aunties about the coins—he has to *give* them the coins—but that he can't tell them about the secret room or the passageways."

"But then . . . where does he say he found the coins?" Misty asked.

"How about he found them in that urn? You know, where the key was?"

"But . . . what if the urn wasn't Mad-Eye Mick's? What if it came from somewhere like the Treasure Emporium?"

"It can't have!" Zelda called over her shoulder. "The key to the secret room was in it!"

"Oh. Oh, right."

"I wonder if anything else that came with the apartment was Mad-Eye's. What if there are other secret hiding places? Like maybe under floorboards or inside walls or . . ."

There was a break in traffic, and when Misty pedaled hard so she could ride next to Zelda, I cut over and put paws to the pavement, too!

"Do you think," Misty said, "that they'll want to take out all the stuff that was there when we moved in? You know, to see if it's got gold hidden in it?"

"I hadn't thought of that!"

"So maybe we *should* tell them about the secret room?"

"No!" Zelda said. "It's the best thing to happen to us since . . . well, since we had to move. And sure, it's their house and there's other stuff back there, but it's not *gold* or probably even very valuable. And the Aunties were risking Dad's life by not calling the police and keeping what they're doing secret!"

"What *are* they doing?" Misty asked.

"I think because the house needs a lot of repairs, it's not legal for them to run a hotel *or* a boarding-house. But they can't afford the repairs or even pay the bills without renters, so they do it anyway. I think that's why they didn't want the police to come over. And I think they make us call them Auntie because the rules are different if *family* lives there."

"Wow," Misty said. "Well . . . the gold should help them a lot, then!"

"It sure should," Zelda said. "But I think we should get *something* out of all this, don't you? So I say we keep the secret room secret."

"Okay," Misty said. "We give them the gold, we keep the secret."

Zelda nodded. "Now we just have to make Dad agree."

Traffic got heavy again, so I ducked back over to the sidewalk and Misty fell into line behind Zelda. They pedaled along without talking for a while, and then Misty said, "We should make up a secret knock."

"One that only we know!" Zelda said, and she seemed excited by the idea.

"So?" Misty called. "What do you want it to be?"

"How about . . . *Knock. Knock-knock*?"

"That's too much like the Evil Overlord's!" Misty said with a laugh.

"Okaaaay," Zelda called over her shoulder, "how about *Knock. Knock-knock. Knock-knock-knock*?"

"One, two, three?"

"Yeah. It's simple and doesn't really *sound* like a secret knock."

"Cool," Misty said, and Zelda grinned like she couldn't wait to use it.

By the time we got back to the Merryweather, I was one tuckered pupper. And thirsty enough to down the *whole* bowl.

The Shenanigans parked their bikes and the Kangaroo Pouch in the shed and hurried to the back door. It smelled like roasting chicken and corn bread.

Scrrrrrrrumptious!

"Aunties?" Zelda called when we were all inside. "Aunties? Where are you?"

Jada and Tiana came charging out of their office. "Where have you *been*?" Jada cried. "We've been worried sick about you!"

"We were rescuing Dad," Zelda said. "He's okay. The kidnappers have been arrested."

"What?" Jada cried. *"How?"*

"Who were they?" Tiana asked. "And *why* did they kidnap him?"

"Did he really have gold coins?" Jada asked.

"It's a long story," Misty said. "Daddy wants us to wait until he gets home so he can explain."

Zelda rushed to add, "He'll be here as soon as he gives his statement to the police." She took a deep breath. "And he . . . he also told us to tell you he needs to talk to you about something. Something important."

"Oh no," Tiana groaned. "Please, girls, it wasn't our fault! Jada didn't know they weren't really FBI agents."

Jada cut in. "And how are we supposed to look after you if you just *vanish* on us?"

"We're sorry," Misty said. "But right now we have to ask—do you want to tell the police about being tied up?"

Jada just stared at her.

"Because, well . . ." Misty side-eyed Zelda. "If you do, you should go to the police station right now."

"We didn't say anything to Dad about it because . . ." Zelda side-eyed Misty. "Because we thought—"

"We thought you should be the one to tell it, since it happened to you," Misty said.

"Hmm . . . ," Jada said, side-eying Tiana.

"That was very . . . *considerate* of you," Tiana said, side-eyeing Jada.

"And why on earth would you think to be so considerate?" Jada asked.

Zelda and Misty gave a shrug.

One that said they'd made off with the butter.

"You girls haven't been *eavesdropping*, have you?" Jada said like a coyote circling a chicken coop.

"Eavesdropping? Us? No!" the Shenanigans said, but it was easy to hear the lie in their voices.

"Oh!" Zelda said, pulling a phone out of her pocket. "Here. One of the kidnappers had it. You said you took pictures of them, so there's proof on here, right?"

Jada took it. "Oh! Thank you for retrieving this!"

Misty added, "So you can call Daddy and meet him at the station if you want to."

"His phone's working?" Tiana asked.

Misty gave me a grin. "Mr. Whiskers retrieved that one."

Tiana blinked at me. Her head shimmied back and forth. Then she hurried to the kitchen drawer, pulled it open, and turned back with her jaw danglin'.

I gave her a pant.

Yip, shoulda listened.

Jada and Tiana had a silent conversation with their eyes, then Tiana said, "I think maybe you girls should go upstairs until your father gets home."

"And this time *stay* up there," Jada said. Then, actin' like I'd never pulled a sock from her mouth or nip-'n'-gnawed her hands free, she said, "And I'm sorry, girls, but Whiskey has to go out."

"But—" Misty said.

"Please," Jada said, pointing to the back door, "put him outside."

So out I went.

Misty brought me a big bowl of water and whispered, "I'm so sorry, boy."

When she was gone, I lapped up every drop, then ambled over to my little shelter. I *was* tuckered out. Maybe more than I'd ever been. But as I rounded the corner of the hedge, I snapped to.

Something smelled . . . different.

I moved closer.

What *was* that?

I crept in.

Sniffed.

Snuffled.

The smell was . . . buttery.

Roasty.

Almost fruity.

And then I found it. Just lyin' there. All by itself.

A full ear of buttered corn.
My heart went happy.
My teeth sank in.
Ah, Sassy.
What a grrrl.

19
Confessions

It was after dark when the Henanigan finally showed up. He went in the back door, as usual. And I slipped in right behind him and hid under the dining room table, as usual.

"Oh, Felix!" I heard Tiana call. "Welcome home! We're so relieved you're all right. We've kept dinner warm. Belle and Brian have already dined, but the girls refused to eat until you returned. They're upstairs." Then she added, "We've waited, too. We thought it would be a nice way to hear about everything that happened."

"Thank you," the Henanigan said. "I *am* famished. I'll go up and get the girls, but it may be a few minutes before we're back."

"That's fine," Tiana said. "We're ready to serve anytime you're ready to eat."

The Aunties hadn't left the house since Zelda returned Jada's phone, so it seemed they'd decided not to make a police report. As a scruffy fella that spends a lot of his time outrunnin' authority myself, I couldn't blame them.

And maybe it was because—even with buttery corn and half the cob in me—my stomach was rumblin' for real food, but it seemed to take the Nanigans a looooong time to come downstairs.

When I finally heard them, I nosed past the tablecloth and saw that the Henanigan was carrying a tote bag. One that looked pretty heavy.

Misty spotted me and hurried to take the seat right in front of me. And as soon as food was served, she started slippin' me bits and pieces, which I wolfed down as quietly as I could.

After everyone had had a few bites to eat, Jada said, "So. Are there really gold coins, Felix? Do they have something to do with your work? From some ancient pharaoh's tomb or something?"

"I'll get to that," the Henanigan said. "But first I

want to apologize for putting everyone here in danger. The girls told me what happened to you, Jada. It sounded awful."

"Well, it wasn't a stroll through the park, I can tell you that," Jada said. "But all's well that ends well, right? I'm over it, and I hope you know we did our best to look after the girls. We were worried sick when we discovered they were gone."

"That wasn't your fault," the Henanigan said. "Not at all."

"So then . . . ," Tiana said, "you're not giving notice?"

"What made you think that?" the Henanigan asked.

"Because Brian did tonight," Tiana answered. "He said he didn't feel safe here. And after what happened to you and how we—"

I saw Jada's foot swipe at Tiana's leg as Jada rushed to say, "He gave notice because of the *noises*. Because it's an *old house*. Because he . . . he heard things today that made him believe in the ghost rumors." She forced a laugh. "Not because of what happened to *you*."

"Silly Mr. Bunker," Misty said.

"Yeah," Zelda added. "Who believes in *ghosts*?"

"Well, I'm glad you girls don't, and I'm glad you're not giving notice," Tiana said. "We know this old place has a lot of . . . *character*, and that it's not for everyone. And we know we have house rules that you girls don't like, but we do try to make it as *homey* as possible."

"We love it here," Misty said.

"Sure do," Zelda added.

"You *do*?" Jada asked.

Tiana laughed. "I would never have guessed that."

"Well, we do," Zelda said.

"Can I have seconds of chicken and corn bread?" Misty asked as she slipped me some food. "I'm super hungry tonight."

"Well, who can blame you?" Tiana said. "You had quite a day!"

I could hear dishes being shifted around, and soon there was a nice juicy chunk of chicken stuck in my muzzle.

"So . . . can we get back to the gold coins, Felix?"

Jada asked. "I'm glad you're not in trouble with the law, but . . . what on earth was this all about?"

Misty slipped me a piece of corn bread with a fat smear of butter.

Scrrrrrumptious!

"Finishing my apology . . . ," the Henanigan said, "I should have come to you straightaway. You see, I found the coins in our apartment."

"You *what*?" Jada asked.

"I . . . I wasn't sure they were real, and I simply wanted to get them authenticated and surprise you. If they *were* as old as they seemed, I thought they might be worth enough to . . . to make a difference around here. But I didn't want to get your hopes up only to dash them."

"But—" Tiana said.

"We know you're having trouble making ends meet," Zelda hurried to add.

"I know now that not telling you right away was wrong," the Henanigan said. "And clearly, it was foolish. Because in my excitement I didn't realize that a phone conversation I was having was being overheard—"

"By the Evil Overlord!" Misty said, slippin' me some more chicken.

"Misty, stop with the 'evil overlord' business," the Henanigan scolded.

"Well, she is," Misty said.

"So the Evil Overlord is a *woman*?" Jada asked. "Does she happen to wear a poufy ponytail?"

"Yes!" Misty said.

"She's the one who tied me up! And stuck a sock in my mouth! A dirty sock, I might add."

"Felix, please," Tiana said. "Get to the point. *Are* they valuable? And where did you find them?"

I saw the Henanigan reach down and lift the funny-footed vase out of his sack. Then it went *thunk* on top of the table, and he asked, "Can you tell me the provenance of this urn?"

"The *provenance* of it?" Jada asked.

"Its history," the Henanigan said. "When you rented me the apartment, you said it came furnished and 'as is.' But the house has been owned by people before you inherited it, and our apartment has been rented to people before us, so . . . do you know anything about this vase or where it came from?"

Maybe I couldn't see Tiana shake her head, but I could sure *feel* it when she said, "It just came with the house." Then she sighed and said, "Maybe we should have gutted the place—really cleaned it up. But we had to pay back taxes and get the roof fixed, and the thought of bringing all of that *stuff* down the stairs was . . . well, we just needed to get it rented."

"Well, here," the Henanigan said, and I could hear the funny-footed base twist off the vase and the coins clink onto the table.

I crept out so I could see what was going on, and there was Jada holdin' her cheeks, and Tiana holdin' both hands against her heart like it might explode. "So . . . *are* they real?" Tiana asked.

"You'll have to bring them into Christie's for verification, but I sent them very clear, very detailed pictures and was told this evening that they do look authentic."

"And . . . ?" Tiana asked, picking up a coin. "Any idea what they're worth?"

The Henanigan lowered his voice. "I'm told that
if they are authentic, they would likely bring in
around a quarter of a million dollars at auction."

"A quarter of a million dollars?!" the Aunties
gasped.

"That's incredible!" Tiana gave the Henanigan a tearful look. "And here you could have just sold them yourself and we would never have known."

"Well, that would've been wrong," the Henanigan said. He took a deep breath. "So . . . balancing everything . . . is it all right if we continue with the arrangement we have? It seems the girls have grown to really like it here, and I would hate to . . . displace them again."

"And if we find any more gold, we'll let you know right away!" Zelda said.

Tiana laughed. "Yes, of course. We would love to have you stay."

Jada grinned. "Assuming you're okay with the *ghosts.*"

Misty and Zelda gave each other secret smiles. "We're fine with them," Misty said with a laugh.

But then Jada caught sight of me and got stern. "I'm sorry, girls. As cute as he is, Whiskey cannot live here."

"But why?" Misty said.

"Do I have to remind you how he tore through

the house this afternoon with that big, snapping dog? It about gave Ms. LeTrist a heart attack!"

"That wasn't—"

"It's house rules, Misty," the Henanigan said. "We agreed to no pets when we moved in, and we need to abide by it." He gave her a firm look. "Put him out. Now."

"I'm so sorry," Misty told me at the back door. "After everything you did today? It's just not fair."

And then Tiana was there, making sure Misty wasn't pullin' any, you know, *shenanigans.* "Say good night," she said.

Misty did.

Then Tiana shut the door.

And locked it up tight.

20
Wait Just a Shake!

I sat at the back door for a little while, staring at it, hoping. But the fog had settled in, and it was chilly outside, so eventually I gave up and went back to my little shelter behind the hedge. I burrowed into some leaves to try to warm up, then gnawed on the rest of my corncob, just to have something to chew on besides how I'd been booted.

Me bein' out in the cold after everything I'd done?

It was just wrrrong.

But it did help that I was tired.

Dog tired.

Pretty soon my eyes were closing and my brain was wanderin' off, thinking about everything that had happened. From my first whiff of Fishy to chasing his car, to finding the Henanigan's phone, to delivering it dripping with superior slobber to Tiana. Then racing upstairs to escape Jada, and Misty letting me inside their apartment, and discovering the key and the moving bookcase and the secret room and the pirate's chest and the gold coins! I remembered how I'd followed the draft to Cawless Crow and how we'd gone down the Doomsday Stairs and walked the planks.

And I was just driftin' off to sleep when my mind reached the Sea Doggy Door.

I snapped awake.

Wait just a shake . . . !

I jumped up, raced over to the Sea Doggy Door, nosed my way in, then ran through the U-turn corridor, past the grate, up the stairs, across the planks, up the second stairs, under Cawless Crow, through the black flag, and into the secret room.

I put an eye up to the crack in the wall.

My tail started whippin' around.

I almost yipped.

The Nanigans were home!

But . . . if I made my move now, it might ruin everything! The Henanigan would just toss me back out.

So I waited.

And watched.

And waited.

And watched.

And finally, when the lights went out and the Henanigan had closed the door to his room, I began scratching on the wall.

Scratch.

Scratch-scratch.

Scratch-scratch-scratch.

I did it over and over and over.

Nobody came.

I did it over and over and over again.

Nobody came.

And I was just gettin' ready to give up when a bit of light came through the wall.

I put my eye up to a crack, and there were Misty and Zelda sneakin' through the living room with a flashlight. "I know what I heard!" Misty whispered.

"It's probably a rat," Zelda said.

"Rats can't count," Misty said.

"And dogs can?"

"This one can," Misty whispered. "And he knows our secret knock."

"That was not a knock. It was creepy scratching!"

"What's he supposed to do? Ram his head against the wall?"

"But how can he know our secret knock? He's just a *dog*."

Misty turned on her sister. "Really? After today that's what you think? That he's just a dog?"

Zelda sighed. "I know, I know. But it's just so unbelievable!"

Scratch.

Scratch-scratch.

Scratch-scratch-scratch.

"He's in the secret room," Misty whispered.

"What if it's *not* him?" Zelda asked, soundin' a little frantic. "What if it's rodents of unusual size—or *any* size?"

"It's him," Misty said. "And I'm letting him in."

Two wags later the lock went *thunk*.

The bookcase shuddered.

And as soon as the opening was wide enough, yippy-yi-*yay*, I leapt through.

I danced around. I was so happy! And I'm afraid a few little yips might've slipped and that my tail was really whippin', because after Zelda had hugged me and ruffled my ears, Misty held my chops in both her hands and whispered, "You have to be quiet, or Daddy will kick you out."

I nodded.

So Zelda filled a bowl of water, and we all crept into the Shenanigans' bedroom. "Here you go, boy," Zelda whispered, placin' the bowl on the floor.

I gave her cheek a lick of thanks, then lapped up a little.

But not too much!

And after Misty pushed away her teddy bears and patted her fuzzy blanket, I jumped up, spun around a few times, and landed in a cushy spot at the foot of the bed.

Misty got under the covers, her smile as big as the one in my heart. Then she leaned forward, tucked me under a blanket, and kissed my forehead. "Sleep tight," she whispered.

Zelda chuckled from under her own covers and whispered, "And don't let the beddy-bugs bite!"

The Shenanigans giggled, and I let out a happy sigh.

It didn't matter what trouble might show up at the door tomorrow.

It didn't matter what other secrets might be buried away in this house.

Tonight I was with the Shenanigans.

Tonight this was home.

It was good to be part of the pack.

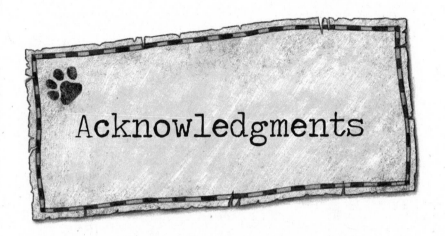

Acknowledgments

Special thanks to my loyal publishing pack, especially Mark, Nancy, and Ginger, and to those at Penguin Random House who have helped whelp this book and shepherd it out into the world.

Also, thanks to Honey Beth Kropp and her students at C.F. Patton Middle School for their insightful feedback on an early version of the manuscript.

And finally, thanks to the dogs who have left a lasting pawprint on my heart, including escape artist Ko-Hii-Ko and his sidekick Thor, faithful and sweet Atushka, Bear the motorcycle pup, harmonizing howlers Kai-Tu and Lassen, switching sentries Bongo and Jazz, and, of course, Sir Bossa the Ridiculous.